A Kiss of Fire

Also by Masako Togawa

The Master Key
The Lady Killer

A Kiss
of
Fire

MASAKO TOGAWA

Translated from the Japanese by

SIMON GROVE

†

DODD, MEAD & COMPANY
New York

TRANSLATOR'S NOTE. At the time when I translated this book, I was under considerable business pressure and requested Gavin Frew to recast points of the translation to make it more suited to English-speaking readers. I wish to thank Mr. Frew profusely for all his work, without which this English-language edition would not have reached its readers in its present form.

—*Simon Grove*

First published in the United States in 1988

Copyright © 1985 by Masako Togawa

Translation copyright © 1987 by Simon Grove

Published by Dodd, Mead & Company, Inc.
71 Fifth Avenue, New York, N.Y. 10003
Manufactured in the United States of America
First Edition

1   2   3   4   5   6   7   8   9   10

Library of Congress Cataloging-in-Publication Data
Togawa, Masako, 1933–
A kiss of fire.
Translation of: Hi no seppun / Togawa Masako.
I. Title.
PL862.03H513   1988   895.6'35   87-19962
ISBN 0-396-09260-8

A Kiss of Fire

PROLOGUE

Extracts from newspapers and magazines of 1958, which gave details of the fire.

The well-known painter, Kazuhiko Matsubara, aged 33, died yesterday in a fire in his home where he was convalescing from an illness. The cause of the fire is unknown but is thought to have been either an electrical short circuit or an unextinguished cigarette.

The son of the painter, Michitaro Matsubara, and two school friends, Ikuo Onda and Ryosaku Uno, unanimously say that they saw a batlike figure run up the stairs of the house, breathing fire. The police, who have not been able to rule out arson, are investigating these claims.

The body of the painter's dog, a terrier named Lulu, was found curled up on the pillow next to its master, and this demonstration of loyalty brought tears to the eyes of everyone who witnessed it.

The rising young star in art circles, Kazuhiko Matsubara, who died recently in a fire, was the eldest son of the founder of the C. D. Insurance Company, Mr. Koichi Matsubara. He studied painting in Paris for ten years and returned to this country last year. He met his wife, Yoriko (30), in France, where she was studying child psychiatry at Paris University. She is presently working as a lecturer at Oyunohara Women's College.

The Fire Department has reached the conclusion that the fire broke out on the second floor in an area where there were no naked lights.

There is a strong possibility that the fire that broke out in the home of the painter, Kazuhiko Matsubara, was caused by three nursery-school children who were playing in the house. The artist's wife, Yoriko, who is a lecturer in child psychiatry at the Oyunohara Women's College, wept as she spoke to our reporter.

"I feel a heavy sense of responsibility, both as a mother and a psychiatrist, to think that my son may have been responsible for the death of my dear husband. It is a cross that we will both have to bear for the rest of our lives, but I don't blame the other children involved at all."

The three children insist that they were not playing with fire in the artist's home and stick to their story of a black, flame-breathing batlike figure, which they claim to have seen running up the stairs.

Yoriko says that she had come home to find the
house already engulfed in flames and says there was
nothing she could do to save her husband. Their dog,
which she had just collected from the vet, ran straight
up to the second floor where her husband was. "My
husband and that dog were devoted to each other,"
Yoriko said, with tears in her eyes.

Several hundred friends and relatives gathered for
the funeral of the late Kazuhiko Matsubara, an up-
and-coming artist and sole heir to the founder of the
C. D. Insurance Company. Many members of the
company called to pay their condolences, but the main
shareholder, the mother of the deceased, did not make
an appearance, and it is rumored that there is discord
within the family.

PART ONE

Twenty-six Years Later

1 *The Fireman*

"Are you leaving already? I'll be lonely without you," Chieko said, putting her arms around him.

"I cannot help that. I've got to go to work." Ikuo spoke in an expressionless voice and hoped that she would not try to make him choose between love and duty. The fact that this was really his night off only made him feel worse.

"But you still have another day off," she said in a soft voice, putting her finger on his weak spot.

He realized that by showing her knowledge of his duty roster like this, she was trying to demonstrate what a good wife she would make for a fireman.

"I can't afford to take long holidays right now, surely you must realize that. The same goes for the men. They haven't caught that arsonist yet. We don't even have time to dry our hoses between fires, which means that when we are called out, we can't respond as quickly as we should. We don't have the time to sit around to recover our energy. We must catch him as soon as possible."

The girl let go of him and kissed him lightly on the chest. She seemed almost convinced.

"We know that he has a pattern. He only strikes on days with a five in them, the days that are consecrated to the fire god. Knowing this, we must go around and warn people about leaving inflammable items near their houses on these days. Everybody is making such a fuss about this arsonist, and yet they can't even be bothered to check that their houses are safe. Half of them deserve to have their houses burned down. They're like teenage girls who insist on sleeping in the nude with the window open when they know there is a rapist on the loose."

No sooner had he spoken than he realized he had chosen an unfortunate example.

"Don't talk about it like that!" she cried, and buried her face in his chest to hide the tears that had sprung to her eyes.

He had forgotten that she had been raped at the age of twelve.

"I'm sorry, I did not mean to put it like that. It's just that everybody behaves as if it could never happen to them, and I have a duty to go out and warn them. This is the most dangerous time. He is like a ghost; he likes to come out around midnight."

He tried to make it into a joke to cheer her up.

"And that is the time I need you the most. As soon as you leave me, I wake up and can't get back to sleep. I sometimes wonder if I am really cut out to be a fireman's wife."

"Don't be ridiculous. You'll make a terrific wife. Now when I leave, just check all the locks and don't leave any-

6

thing inflammable lying around, especially cardboard boxes. The bastard has a special weakness for cardboard boxes."

"All right, I'll lock the doors after you leave, and if I can't get to sleep, I will take some sleeping pills."

"How many times must I tell you? Whatever you do, you must not take any sleeping pills." He glanced down at his watch. It was ten minutes to twelve. The longer he stood here arguing with his girl, the less chance he had of catching the arsonist.

"Don't worry, the doctor made them up for me. They are only light tranquilizers. They're not addictive."

"That's not the point. Don't you understand what is happening? This bastard is no longer content with just setting things on fire. Every time he strikes he leaves at least one dead body behind him."

"But he's not likely to come around here."

"That's what you think. He has been gradually expanding his territory, and he could easily choose this area for his next attack. Unless you want to wake up dead one morning, you had better lay off the sleeping pills, at least until we catch him."

He was too worried about the passing of time; he should have taken longer to explain the situation; he should have made it appear that it was her own idea to stop taking the tranquilizers until the arsonist was caught, but it was too late for that now. She lost her temper and turned on him in a rage.

"Do this, do that. You think that everything can be solved by rules, but life is not as easy as that. There are such things as pain, you know, and medicines to cure it. If you really must know, the reason that I can't sleep at night is because I suffer from bad stomach cramps. The doctor knows all about it. That is why he gave me those pills. You can ask him if you don't believe me."

"I realize that you need to take the pills. I am just saying that now is not the time."

"Don't exaggerate. You always look on the worst side of everything. Just because you forget to lock a door, it doesn't mean that an arsonist is going to burn you out of house and home. You blow up the smallest event and make it sound like a disaster. I think you enjoy trying to scare people."

She drew away from him, and he could see the anger smoldering in her eyes. He knew he should take the time to talk to her and make her realize that he only spoke to her as he did because he worried about her, but instead he looked at his watch. It was twelve o'clock.

"Your trouble is that you are too careless. If you had been a bit more careful when you were twelve, you would never have had to suffer that terrible experience."

He had meant to try to reason with her, but for some reason he had said the one thing he should not have said.

"What do you know about anything? You are a cold, callous man. I can't live with someone like you. I could never have your children. It's all over between us."

She turned her back on him, sobbing and waiting for him to reach out to her and make up. But he ignored her silent plea and pulled on his jeans, tucking his shirt into them. He was filled with anger and was not in the mood to sympathize with her.

If only he was to take his days off, he would now be in bed with this girl, making love, and would soon be dropping into an exhausted sleep, but instead, here he was, going out into the night to continue his solitary patrols through the frozen streets. He knew that the chances of his actually catching the arsonist red-handed were minimal, but he felt driven to try anyway.

At the entrance to the apartment building, he found a cardboard box that had been used to deliver some fruit to someone in the building. It was half-filled with rice chaff that had been used as packing, which was quite unusual these days, but something that the arsonist was particularly fond of. All it would take was some gasoline and a match and *whoosh*! The old wooden apartment building would go up like a torch and be reduced to ashes in less than an hour.

And what of Chieko? She had taken her sleeping pills and would never know what happened. Her white body that had so recently hugged him close, her red lips that had been twisted with rage as she shouted at him—all would be destroyed.

He picked up the box and began to move it to a safe place, but then he brought it back and put it down where he had found it. For the first time since he had graduated from the fire academy, he was acting contrary to all his training.

She accused me of being petty and overcareful, but if this box catches fire, we'll soon see who was in the right. I'll be damned if I'm going to move it.

He kicked the box with the toe of his jogging shoe and set off into the deserted streets. He wondered absently if his foe, walking silently through the frozen streets, was also wearing jogging shoes.

Chieko had always whispered "My fireman" in his ear as he left on his patrol, but tonight had been different, and he felt a pang of sadness sweep through him.

2   *The Arsonist*

It was like a large, black shadow. It had two arms, two legs, and a huge bloated head. In the dim light of the street lamps, it looked almost like a gigantic black tadpole. Like a tadpole, it moved soundlessly as it flitted from shadow to shadow in search of its prey.

He was searching for some of those empty cardboard boxes that he liked so much, and the reason that he moved so soundlessly was, as the fireman had suspected, because he was wearing thick-soled jogging shoes. He was carrying a plastic bag full of gasoline around his neck, which was why his head looked so bloated. All he had to do was fling the bag against the corner of one of those cardboard boxes he liked so much, and it would burst open to soak everything in gasoline.

The mere smell of the gasoline is enough to make his whole body tremble, but it is nothing like the feeling that grips him when he throws a lighted match onto the gasoline. When he hears the bang of the explosion and watches the blue flames lick up into the night air, he is gripped by what can only be called an orgasm. His body becomes rigid and he feels as if his spirit is floating up to heaven for a moment, until the realization of what he has done grips him and plunges his soul into hell. Now the black shadow disappears like the wind into the night—like a black wind that can never be caught.

One day they will catch him, though, all those people whose loved ones and memories he has turned into ashes. They will not forgive him his shuddering ecstasies, and he knows it. For not much longer would he enjoy the embrace of the flames, the sweet kisses of fire. Already someone is on his trail.

He knows that now is the time to stop, to bring an end to this evil, but he can't. He will never be able to stop until they catch him.

3   *The Fireman*

Ikuo found the cardboard boxes in the garden, piled up against the wooden walls of the old house like kindling for a fire. The boxes appeared to have been sent from overseas and still had an address written on them in English. He could not make out the surname, but he could read the first name, "Mitsuko," as it was the same as the French perfume that Chieko used.

He went up to the door and pressed the button of the intercom.

"Hello, I'm from the fire brigade. . . ."

He was answered by a surly woman's voice speaking a foreign language.

"There is an arsonist on the loose in this area, so please do not leave any inflammables by . . ."

Before he had a chance to finish what he was saying, he

was interrupted by the woman's angry voice echoing from the loudspeaker of the intercom. This time she was using Japanese and spoke in the same hysterical tones that Chieko had used when he had left.

"What the hell do you think you are talking about? This is my garden, so kindly mind your own business! Can't you see that I have only just moved into this house, so for God's sake shut up about it burning down."

"You may not realize it," he said patiently, keeping his temper under control, "but this road is too narrow for a fire truck to pass through, so if your house were to catch fire it would spread to the surrounding buildings before we could get it under control."

"You don't know what you are talking about. This house is built on a very lucky spot. I had a fortuneteller come and check it out, and he told me that it was the perfect position for a building, so don't give me any of this rubbish about arsonists. Are you really a fireman? Show me your identification. What are you thinking of, waking people in the middle of the night. I'm going to call the police." She sounded drunk and was shouting now.

"I quite understand. I'm sorry to have bothered you, but couldn't you just put these boxes indoors for tonight? I'll help you."

He looked down at the boxes, which had obviously been used in a move from abroad—cardboard boxes, just the kind that the bastard liked the most, and today was a day with a five in it—the twenty-fifth! That bastard had been quiet for a month now, but would he be able to hold himself back for another week? Ikuo did not think so. He could understand the desires boiling in his adversary's heart almost as if they were his own, and he knew that tonight was the night. If he saw this mountain of cardboard, he would not be able to resist it any longer. He would be drawn to this spot like a moth to the light.

Suddenly the front door was flung open, and he was confronted by a woman of about thirty. Her negligee hung open to expose her breasts, and her eyes were bloodshot.

"Just what do you think you are doing? This is my house, and that is my garden, and I will keep what I like in it. What makes you think that you have the right to tell me where to keep my rubbish?

"Now how about showing me some identification. You don't look like a fireman to me, dressed like that. Look at your dirty jeans and jogging shoes. Call yourself a fireman? I wouldn't be surprised if you were the arsonist yourself. I've heard of your type before, a match in one hand and a hose in the other. You start the fire and then try to get the credit for putting it out afterward."

He did not answer her but bent down to pick up the boxes, telling himself that no matter how obnoxious she may be, she would become a charred corpse if he did not clear away all the cardboard.

The woman came toward him and struck him in the chest, knocking the boxes out of his hands.

"You can just leave those where they are. Don't think that just because I am a woman you can do what you like. Now show me your identification, or I really will call the police."

She grabbed him violently by the lapels.

He reached into the back pocket of his jeans for the black leather wallet where he kept his I.D. and driver's license, but it was not there. He was sure that he had picked it up when he left Chieko's apartment, but maybe he had forgotten it in his hurry.

When the woman saw him hesitate, she hit him in the face.

"You liar! You are the arsonist! Well, if you're going to start a fire, do it now with me watching you. Come on, what's keeping you? Are you scared? I bet this doesn't work either," she said, grabbing his crotch. "Impotent, that's what you are."

She carried on her tirade in a foreign language that sounded like French, then broke into raucous laughter. Looking at this drunken woman with her heavy veined breasts hanging out of her open negligee, he suddenly lost his temper.

All it would take is a good dousing with gasoline and a match and the world would be rid of her, he thought. *If nobody else does it, I would be tempted to do it myself.*

Nevertheless, he managed to keep his temper under control. Picking up the boxes again, he started to put them inside the porch. The woman stepped back, and that was when he noticed the cage. It was a big cage like the ones used in the circus to house lions, and, sure enough, this one also contained a large lion with a flowing mane.

"You impotent bastard, I'll feed you to my lion. That will teach you to pass yourself off as a fireman. Arsonist! Murderer! Rapist!"

He gave up and walked away, leaving the woman laughing hysterically in the midst of her mountain of boxes. She and her pet lion could be burned to death for all he cared. He was hurt and felt sick of women, but despite his anger he paused in the dark gateway of an apartment about one hundred yards from the woman's house. He knew only too well that if the woman's house caught fire, it would spread to this building before it could be brought under control. The fire precautions in this area were not what were to be expected for the capital city of an advanced country.

It was only his strong sense of duty that made him stay on and guard the woman's house, but when one of the neighbor's dogs started to bark at him he gave up and moved on. He felt like a fool for conducting these solitary patrols when all they brought him was grief, and after walking back to the main road he took a taxi home. He drank a couple of whiskies before going to bed. Then, driving out all thought of the arsonist, his girl, and the madwoman with the lion, he fell asleep.

Thirty minutes after Ikuo left, a black shadow shaped like a tadpole appeared in the very same gateway where Ikuo had kept his solitary vigil. When the shadow moved, the only sound that could be heard was the slopping of the gasoline in the bag around his neck.

4   *The Fireman*

Ikuo looked sleepily at the report in the evening paper as he made his way to the fire station. He was over the worst of the shock he had felt that morning when he saw the flames burning on the television news. Indeed, he was over the shock, but not the chagrin and anger, and he ground his teeth helplessly.

If only he had stayed on guard for a little longer. He had known in his bones that the bastard would turn up, so why had he left? Could it have been that he had secretly hoped that the woman and her pet lion would die? There was no point in worrying about it now, but would the bastard ever appear again? Last night he had reaped his greatest harvest yet, and surely that would be enough even for him. First there was the French woman and her pet lion, then there was the old couple in the apartment next door. They were aged eighty-seven and seventy-nine and were bedridden, so it might even have been a blessing for them to die together in their sleep, but it was not a blessing for the young mother who had died with her baby in her arms, leaving two primary-school children to fend for themselves. No wonder the people's anger against the arsonist had reached new heights.

The drunken woman with the lion had brought it on herself, but the innocent baby that had perished was blameless, and Ikuo had to bear some of the responsibility for it. He knew the arsonist was going to turn up, but still he had gone away. Surely he had to share the responsibility, even indirectly.

If he carried on thinking like this it would destroy him, but he could not help it. He had been haunted by such thoughts since the age of five. He could still remember striking those matches and watching them drop to the floor, tiny seeds of flame that had grown until they became an inferno, which had left a charred corpse in its wake. His hands had been responsible for a fire.

"I could have been killed!" Chieko had sounded almost hysterical when she rang him that morning. The night before, she had scorned him for warning her about leaving boxes lying around and taking sleeping pills, but now, a few short hours later, she was on the line blaming him as if it had been his fault.

"Soon after you left, a cardboard box outside my window caught fire, and, if it had not been for the boy who lives in the room opposite, I might have been burned to death. It's all your fault. You knew about it, but you left it there to burn!"

"Don't exaggerate. One cardboard box is not likely to burn down a building like yours. He was only trying to divert our attention. He had planned to burn down that house with the lion all along."

He was convinced of that. At least he knew that his girl would not die in a fire. Thinking of her, he remembered the sex they had enjoyed the night before and the moment of their orgasm.

"How do you know that?" She was silent for a few minutes, then said, "I know, you went past that house on your patrol, didn't you?"

"Yes, I went past it."

"Well, if you saw all those boxes, why didn't you tell her to clear them away? Oh, I see, you wanted to make an example of her for me, didn't you?"

"Don't be ridiculous. Of course I told her to clear them away," he answered in a bored voice. He could see that whatever he said, she was going to accuse him of putting his job before her again.

"So you warned her, and yet you left that box outside my apartment. Did you want me to be killed? Have you tired of me already?"

"Don't be so ridiculous," he said helplessly.

"I bet it was you who set the fire. I bet you are the arsonist!"

"If I was, it wouldn't say much for your taste in men, would it? First a rapist and then an arsonist."

He spoke in a cold voice. Only the night before, that drunk woman had said the same thing. Would Chieko's feelings for him take precedence, or would she persist in her accusations? He waited for her to speak.

"I'm sorry, I didn't mean it. You're not that kind of man. I love you more than anything!" Her voice trembled as she stifled a sob.

"But maybe it is me. Maybe I am the arsonist. Don't you remember that movie we saw on TV the other week, what was it called? *Psycho*, wasn't it? Maybe I have a split personality like the hero in that movie, and the arsonist that I am hunting is really me."

"Of course it isn't you. It's impossible." He could hear a hint of doubt creep into her voice. "But last night you said you were on duty when really it was your day off. And soon after you left, that box under my window caught fire. Now, come to mention it, all the big fires have occurred on your nights off."

The doubt in her voice changed to fear.

"It's true. The fires always occur on my days off, when I am out patrolling on my own, and they always occur in the very area that I choose to patrol that day. If it happens again, I won't be able to put it down to coincidence anymore. Maybe I am a sort of Jekyll and Hyde, the top graduate from the fire academy by day and an arsonist by night."

18

"Stop it! Don't talk like that. I don't believe it could be you!"

"I don't want to believe it either, but sometimes I have my doubts. It helps to be able to talk to you like this."

"You must stop patrolling on your own on your nights off. You don't even get paid for it. You should rest while you have the chance. You should spend your nights off with me, in my arms, not walking the cold streets."

"And what if there are no more fires? Do you want me to spend the rest of my life wondering if it was me who killed all those people?"

"I don't care, I will never let you go, I love you."

"But can't you see, I will never be able to rest until I have caught him. I have to catch him with my own hands, and I can't stop now when I am so close."

"And what if it is you? You are going to be putting the noose around your own neck."

"If that's the case, then so be it."

"So you don't love me then!"

"That's not true, but this is a personal problem, one that I have had since I was five."

She was not listening to him anymore. Nobody understood him, not her, not anyone, and yet they did not hesitate to blame him when they thought it suited them. The evening newspaper that he was reading seemed to blame the fire brigade for not doing something about the arsonist, as if that was their job. Folding the paper, he got off the train and made his way toward the fire station.

"It's all right for some," one of his colleagues said cheerfully as he walked in. "You always seem to have your night off when there is a big fire to deal with. Oh, by the way, the chief was looking for you."

He walked through to the chief's room, and as he entered, the chief, who was on the verge of retirement, fixed him with a stern eye.

"And where were you last night, may I ask?"

5   The Detective

Detective Ryosaku Uno started to walk down the steep hill, and as he did so, he reflected on the fact that hills could only really be called steep when they were being climbed. Descending them was quite another matter. He had attended junior high school in Nagasaki where many of the hills were horrendously steep, but he always found that once he reached the top, the view had made it worth the effort.

He had been so busy with his thoughts that he had walked straight past the temple, which was the object of his visit. He paused at the bottom of the hill while he tried to build up his energy to go back up, and as he did, he looked at a sign that had been placed there by the local educational committee. It was obviously there for the benefit of tourists, and it was fashioned to resemble placards used in ancient times.

This road is known as Bandit's Hill . . .

He read that, three hundred years before, it had been the haunt of a gang of bandits who posed as palanquin bearers and robbed the unlucky travelers who hired them to help them up the hill. Brought back to the present by a crowd of brightly dressed young women who came out of a nearby chocolate factory, he began walking up the hill.

He had been married three years earlier and had spent his honeymoon in San Francisco, another city that was famous for its hills, but six months after his wedding his wife had died in a traffic accident, and ever since he had felt cut off from the people around him. He could no longer find himself motivated to sit for the promotion exams like his rivals at the station, and he did not even enjoy singing in bars after work like they did.

Recently his boss had tried to interest him in remarrying and had shown him lots of pictures of healthy looking college graduates with tennis rackets clutched to their breasts, but he did not find himself at all interested.

There was only one thing that did interest him, and that was the search for the arsonist.

I'll catch him with my own hands, he thought. Although he was attached to the team that was charged with investigating the fires, he was not supposed to let his own feelings interfere with his judgment, but he could not help it.

He walked halfway back up the hill until he came to a temple gateway with the name *Kaenji, the Temple of Flames*, written on it. It was obviously a temple of some antiquity, and although it was not very large, it was beautifully looked after. Apart from several believers who were there to pray, he also observed a number of tourists, cameras in hand, who had come to explore the grounds.

The tourists did not seem to be so interested in the temple buildings, which dated from the feudal period, or in the

21

magnificent three-hundred-year-old plum tree, but rather
in a group of one hundred, moss-covered, stone Buddhas,
which stood on the hillside to the left of the temple buildings. They had been designated as important cultural assets,
but due to land subsidence over the years they were all
standing at different angles. He realized that the sign he
had noticed at the entrance of the temple protesting the
construction of high-rise buildings in the area had been put
there in an effort to protect these statues.

When he had been brought here as a boy, his hand held
firmly by an adult, he had never dreamed that he would
live to see the day when this temple would be overshadowed
by tall buildings. The group of statues had seemed as big
as mountains, a panorama to rival the Himalayas, but now
the little figures at his feet were just another group of
Buddhas. While the group of figures, each with a different
expression, were quite remarkable, they had seemed much
more frightening in those days, like devils.

The adult who held his hand so firmly had threatened
him and said, "It was you who started that fire, wasn't it?
Come on, tell the truth. If you are honest, you will be
forgiven, but if not, these Buddhas will come and tear out
your tongue."

"It wasn't me! It wasn't me!" he had screamed as he
struggled to free his hand. But had he been telling the
truth, or had he just been terrified of being called a criminal?

He felt the sweat run down his armpits just as it had
twenty-six years before. Why had that grown-up tried to
scare a child in such a way? He looked at the statues
again. The adult had said that if he was lying, the statues
would come to him at night and scatter hot coals on his

face. He had had nightmares about it for several months, until he entered primary school, and every time he did, he wet his bed.

His thoughts were interrupted by the excited voice of a middle-aged woman, acting as if she was still a schoolgirl.

"Did that many people really die in one night in fires? It sounds very scary. I'm glad that I didn't live in those days."

"That's nothing," said the elderly man who was with her. It was easy to see from the way they were behaving that they were having an affair. "Those fires might have been big by medieval standards, but they were nothing compared to the air raids in the last war. The incendiary bombs fell like rain, and thousands died in one night, not hundreds. If you were to make a statue of each of the people who died then, you would need a lot more space than this."

"Really, that's terrible. But one thousand people or one, death by fire is horrible. I hope they find that arsonist soon. That's one crime I can't forgive."

"Yes, they will have to make a temple for arson victims at this rate, and they will have to put a statue of a lion in among all the other Buddhas," the man answered coldly.

Ryosaku left the couple and walked through to the back of the temple. If his memory served him right, there was a statue there that had been new twenty-six years ago. The adult had taken him to it and tried to force him to admit that he had started the fire.

"Look, even though you started the fire, the victim has become a Buddha and will forgive you, but first you must admit everything, otherwise . . ."

"No! It wasn't me!"

23

He arrived at the spot where the statue should have been, only to find that another had taken its place. It was a brand-new marble statue of a lion, and he stood staring at it for some time as he tried to think who could have put it there and for what purpose. Gradually it dawned on him that it must have been put there by the arsonist or by someone who knew him well.

He decided that he must get a photograph of the new statue, but as he started to walk away he noticed a sign saying that permission was needed to photograph the statues. He decided that he would keep the temple out of his inquiries for as long as possible. He had only come here by chance, and he could not afford to let the arsonist know that he was on his trail.

6 *The Arsonist*

Michitaro Matsubara sat at the breakfast table, tearing his toast into small pieces and soaking it in low-fat milk before trying to force it down his throat, but he was not doing very well. It was always like this the next morning.

The morning after he had started a fire, he always found it difficult to eat his toast, but today was even worse than usual. Perhaps it was because of the mistake he had made the night before. He should have been a bit more prudent, but he got carried away and acted without thinking. It would have been better if he had postponed the whole thing. That lion had been too dangerous. People might even begin to guess at his real motives.

He shook his head and read the morning papers. The fire had been started too late to appear in the morning press, and although it would probably be on the morning news, his mother made a habit of turning off the TV before they started a meal. Being an expert on child psychiatry, she thought it was her duty to make a good example for her son, but over the years it had become a habit with her.

"No appetite this morning? You don't have to eat anything if you don't want to," she said as if she knew just what was on his mind. She had spoken to him like this since he was three. "If you don't want to do something, nobody is going to force you; you are a free person," she would say. Or, "Just because you are the grandson of the founder of a major insurance company, it does not mean that you have to take over the business. It is entirely up to you."

In this way she had bound him to her will. With a glance she would tell him that if he wanted to rebel against her that was his right, but if he did she would withhold an equal amount of love from him. Her power over him hadn't diminished in the least, and even though he was now thirty-one years old he found himself powerless to break away.

"I'm hungry, it's just . . ."

"It's just what? Oh, I know. It's that girl you're going to meet today, isn't it? Well, you had better go and see her. You know what your aunt is like; she is always trying to marry people off, and she has gone to a lot of trouble to arrange this. If you don't like the girl, nobody is going to force you to date her. But if you like her, why not? It is about time you got married."

"I don't want to get married yet," he said, avoiding her gaze.

He found that as soon as he said this, the toast that had lodged in his throat until then slid down his throat with ease. It was quite simple. There was no need to worry. He would remain single and continue to live with his mother always. That would solve all his problems.

"No, you must get married. I have never asked anything of you before, but I am now. Promise me that you will get married within the year. If you don't, people will say that I have tied you to my apron strings, and I will become a laughingstock."

She sat looking at him, her hands resting lightly in her lap and looking every inch an academic. She had published a book of his correspondence with her while he was in junior high, which had become a best seller, and the photograph of her on the back cover was identical to the way she looked now.

"Yes, it would be bad for business, wouldn't it," he said. His mother always referred to psychiatry as a business. She said that while she may have married the son of a millionaire, she wanted to make her own mark on the world and that education was her way to accomplish this.

"That's quite right. I got where I am on my own, and I don't owe anyone anything. I may have married well, but that has no bearing on my life now, and you would do well to be the same. You must decide what you want out of life, and then choose a suitable partner to help you get it."

A successful insurance man? No, they were sure to find

him out sooner or later, and although famous scholars would be able to expound on his motives for years to come, it would all be over for him. The newspapers and television would brand him as a wolf in sheep's clothing, an arsonist disguised as an insurance man, and he would never be able to hold a good job again.

"O.K. I'll meet the girl, but I want you to come with me," he said resignedly.

"Don't be ridiculous. You can't remain a mama's boy forever. I most certainly will not go. It is up to you to decide."

She trembled slightly as she spoke. She had been a great beauty in her prime, and although she was now fifty-six, for a moment she looked more like a woman in her thirties.

He knew she was struggling to hide her jealousy and that she would never forgive him if he went to see this girl alone. He could never take up with girls seriously or get married, he thought, for, after all, his mother had given up any chance of remarriage in order to devote herself to him. The only way he could ever have any freedom would be to break with his mother altogether, but he did not have the strength to do that.

"I mean it. I have never asked anything of you before, but I am asking it now," his mother said, repeating herself.

Suddenly he realized that she was wrong. When he was five years old, she had asked him to do something. She had taken his hands in hers and fixed him with an intense gaze.

"It was not you who started the fire. It was not you who struck the matches, all right? It definitely was not you."

He was struck dumb by her threatening glare.

27

"If it really was you, tell your mother. Come on, tell me the truth."

He realized that she really did want him to admit that it was he. She wanted him to take all the blame.

"Yes, I struck the matches. I went to Daddy's bed and struck the matches. I thought it would be like the little match girl in the story, that we would be able to see all the Christmas presents, the castle, and the horses. I never dreamed that it would start a big fire or that Daddy would be killed."

It was a brilliant defense for a boy of five, but his mother grabbed him by the shoulders and shook him, shouting, "Why do you insist on lying to me like that? You could not have started the fire. There were two other boys there. It had to be one of them. It was not you. Admit it. It wasn't you! If anyone asks you, the police or your teachers at school, you must not say that it was you. O.K.? I will never ask you anything again, but I am asking you now. You must never say that it was you who started that fire."

For the first time in his short life, he found himself terrified of his mother. How could she see through his lies so easily? Of course it had not been he who had played with the matches and started the fire, but he felt that she wanted him to say that it was.

"It was me, Mummy. I started the fire."

Her response was to hit him hard on the cheek. It was the first time she had ever hit him.

"Don't talk nonsense. It could not have been you!"

He felt as if he had gone deaf, but he would never forget the anger he saw burning in her eyes as she spoke.

28

7   The Fireman

Ikuo stood stiffly at attention in front of his chief. He always found it difficult to talk normally to a superior.

"Last night. . .?" he stammered in answer to the Chief's question.

Where was he? What was he doing? Since when did the Chief have the right to question him about what he did when he was off duty?

Should he be honest and say that he was with his girl, a nurse from the university hospital who wanted to marry him, that they were in bed together? Should he describe her as just his girlfriend, or should he say that she was his fiancée? Either way, the Chief was not likely to approve, as he wanted Ikuo to marry his daughter.

"Last night . . ." he stammered again.

"Don't get me wrong, I'm not criticizing you. What you do on your nights off is entirely up to you, but not if you continue to act as a fireman on your own time. Let's be frank. You told someone to move a pile of cardboard boxes that was stacked up in front of her house last night, didn't you? That's what I mean by acting as a fireman. You were overheard arguing with the woman by someone in the apartment next door. She was pretty drunk, wasn't she?"

"I cannot say whether she was drunk or not, but she would not follow my advice."

"Do you always use that road?"

"No . . ." he stammered again. He hated himself for not being able to speak properly to his superiors and shook his head slightly before coming back to attention.

"You are the best fireman that I have got, and I realize you have been spending your days off patrolling the streets on your own in an effort to reduce the damage being caused by this arsonist."

The Chief gave a sigh as if to say that he wished he could do the same. He took out his silver lighter to light a cigarette, but then put it back in his pocket without using it.

"Do you think our firebug uses a lighter or matches? When he first started causing all these fires, I swore that I wouldn't have a cigarette until he was caught, and as a result I have been able to give up all together." He seemed to be saying this to calm himself down rather than to put his subordinate at ease. "Don't mind me though. You can smoke if you like."

"No thank you. I don't."

Ikuo felt awkward. With nothing to do with his hands, he slipped one into his pocket where he felt the shape of a cheap plastic lighter he had been given at a coffee bar. He had meant to give it to his girl, but had forgotten. He thought of her smoking in bed. She must smoke at least fifty cigarettes a day, and it was enough to put him off marrying her. Smoking was bad for the unborn, and on top of that she took sleeping pills regularly. He could not understand why girls insisted on doing things like that when they knew they would have children one day. His girl, in particular, was a nurse and should know better than anyone the dangers involved in smoking, but whenever he cautioned her about it, she would scowl and make it obvious that she did not want him to criticize her.

"I was born to live my own life, not just to have children."

He realized that he did not have the right to criticize her, but it always upset him that after they had made love, she would slip a cigarette into those same lips that had caressed him a few moments before. Thinking of her lips on his body, he felt a thrill go through him, and he wondered if he would ever be able to leave her, although he realized that he had to.

"What is your opinion? Personally, I sometimes think he does it with a flint and steel, a magic flint with a curse engraved on it."

Although he realized that his superior was joking, he took a pace forward and answered seriously.

"No, personally I think he uses matches."

"Matches? Yes, it is true that we find a lot of burnt matches at the scene of his fires. They are a kind of trademark of his, but I wonder why. Do you think he uses damp matches or do you think he keeps striking the matches but hesitates before he actually lights the fire?

"When people commit suicide, they usually inflict several superficial wounds while they try to key themselves up to make the fatal one. The police think that our pyromaniac may be similar. He stands there lighting one match after another while he struggles with his conscience."

He hit his desk irritably and took a pack of vitamin C tablets from his drawer. He was still having trouble giving up cigarettes. "That's what the investigation division says, anyway."

Ikuo gave a sigh. He did not know much about that kind of thing, but the investigation division employed all kinds of psychologists and experts, and if they said that was the

case he was quite prepared to believe them. He knew that
if he was the arsonist, he would stand there striking match
after match and watching the flame until it burned down
to his fingers. Just like the little match girl in the story,
he would strike match after match until the box was empty.
That was how it had been twenty-six years ago when he
and the other five-year-olds had played with fire.

"I suppose that is one way of looking at it, but I am not
so sure. I think that he is more shrewd and calculating, like
a cat slinking in the shadows." Ikuo was surprised that he
could talk so easily when it came to the subject of the
arsonist, but he felt very strongly about it. It seemed as
though the bastard had appeared the moment that he had
finished his patrol.

"Yes, but catching him is a job for the police," said the
Chief. "You may be an excellent fireman, but I don't want
you to try to capture him on your own and grab all the
glory for yourself."

"I didn't . . ."

"The ordinary man in the street is even more upset about
all this than we are. They are the victims, and as a result
they are scared and panicky. They don't try to understand
your motives like I do. In fact, the people in the house next
to that fire yesterday are saying it was your fault. They say
that when you warned that woman about the boxes, you
purposely tried to annoy her, and then later you set fire to
the boxes to teach her a lesson. Can't you see that this is
just the kind of thing the press has been waiting for, and
you've only got yourself to blame? An old lady in an apartment nearby says that she saw the fire start and says that it

was done by a man dressed like a bat who breathed fire, but obviously nobody takes her seriously."

"Maybe I was a bit blunt with that woman last night, but now I wish that I had kept up my watch all night," Ikuo replied with his head bowed. The old woman must be going senile to come out with a story like that, but it was strange that she should say the same thing that he and his friends had said when they were children. After all, it had been a lie . . . or had it? Hadn't they really seen a batlike man breathing flames?

"Why did you drop your I.D. card and driver's license?" The Chief's question brought him back to the present. He had forgotten all about them, but now he remembered that they had been missing the night before.

"Have they been found?"

"Yes, they were found in the stomach of the lion. It broke out of its cage with its coat on fire, and the police had to shoot it. They performed an autopsy afterward and found your wallet, but how do you think it got there?" The Chief sounded quite amazed.

"I don't know; I have no idea," he replied weakly. He was as astounded as his chief.

8 *The Detective*

The detective did not believe in Providence or fate. He believed that everything happened by chance. The traffic accident that killed his wife, the fact that she had been pregnant with their first child when she died—it was all mere chance. He firmly believed that all these things were completely devoid of any other meaning.

That is why he made no comment at the investigation conference when he heard that a fireman's wallet had been found in the stomach of the lion that had died in the fire. Yet when he heard that an old woman insisted that she had seen a batlike man breathing fire on the pile of cardboard boxes, he found that he could not join in his colleagues' laughter. It awoke memories of his childhood when he and his friends had told a similar childish lie.

The name on the fireman's documents was Ikuo Onda, and that also stirred a memory somewhere in his subconscious, but he did not stop to worry about it.

After the conference, he had a sudden urge to eat some grilled eel, so he went to a little eel restaurant nearby. He was in the middle of his meal when the name "Ikuo" came back to him. Ikuo had been the name of his best friend at nursery school, and they had always done everything together. Ikuo's father had owned a small laundry, while his own father ran a newspaper shop nearby. Neither of them had had mothers so they had felt a strong attraction for each other, but he could not remember if his friend's family name had been Onda or not. He tried to remember what the teacher at school had called him or what had been the name that was written on the badge he had worn, but his memory failed him. All he could remember was that he had greeted the other boy as Ikuo. He wondered if his birthday had been on January the second, but it was no good, he could not remember. It was probably only a coincidence that the fireman had the same name as his childhood friend, but it had been enough to dredge up memories of his old friend, memories that he had tried so hard to forget. It may have been because of the old woman's story about a fire-breathing man, but he did not think so. It was mention of the fireman's name that did it.

Now that he thought about it, he remembered that when they had been playing with fire, it had been Ikuo who had always burst into tears and put the fire out when it started to spread. They would become scared of the flames and the smoke and run outside, but Ikuo remained behind and doused the flames. As a result, he was always the one who got caught by the grownups and punished, but that did not stop him. That had been before the big blaze when someone died. They had always been playing with matches during that period in their lives.

Ikuo stayed behind to put out the fires, and it may be that he had been cut out to be a fireman even at that tender age. Of course, it had not been Ikuo who was responsible for the fires, the detective thought wryly. That had been himself.

There was nothing to be gained by thinking of it now. There were any number of people of his age called Ikuo, and it seemed very unlikely that the fireman could be his old childhood friend. But if the fireman was not his childhood friend, why did the Chief Inspector call him and inform him of the discovery of the documents in the lion?

Up until now the arsonist had been responsible for at least twenty fires, and ten people had died in them, but he had never left a clue as to his identity. All that they knew was that he had a strange attraction to cardboard boxes.

Ryosaku guessed that his superior had decided that the fireman's wallet contained the first real clues they had and wanted him to follow up on the discovery.

The detective finished lunch.

They had Ikuo Onda's driver's license and I.D., which meant that they had only the bare facts: his name, age, and address, but that was all. No matter how hard they might study these facts, they could never learn the details that brought the flesh-and blood man to life, his private existence, his academic record, and his childhood memories. Nevertheless, they had a good start.

Onda's apartment turned out to be in an old, concrete apartment block. There was a concierge, but he did not seem to know anything about the tenants, most of whom were single. The detective went up to Onda's room and saw the morning paper sticking out of the mail slot in the door, natural enough as Onda was on duty that day. The concierge, who had followed him up, pushed the paper through the slot.

"Mr. Onda sometimes complains that his newspaper gets stolen," he said. "As you know, he is a fireman, and when he works the night shift he sometimes comes home to find that his paper is missing. I think that it is probably someone in the building, but I can't do anything about it until I catch them. I don't know what the world is coming to. I know that the price of the paper has gone up recently, but that's no excuse to go stealing other people's."

Ryosaku also had his paper stolen sometimes, so he knew how it felt. If only the newsboy would just take a little more trouble and push the paper all the way through the door, there would be no problem. But having a father who operated a newspaper shop, he had also delivered papers as a boy and so he also sympathized with the newsboys.

"Do Mr. Onda's papers ever pile up for a few days?" he asked pointedly.

"Not as a rule, but sometimes when his days off fall at the weekend they build up for a couple of days. I don't think he comes home, but I can't say for sure."

The concierge had seen Ryosaku's police identification, so he answered the question carefully.

"Do you have any idea where he stays? Has he given you a number where you can contact him in case of emergency?" He decided that it would be worth stopping off at the local police call box on his way back and checking the patrol records.

"I ask all my tenants to give me a number, but most of them seem to think that it is too much bother. Not Mr. Onda though; he always lets me know."

Ryosaku followed the concierge back to his office and looked at the address. The address was under a woman's name, and he realized that it was near the house where the lion had been. Perhaps he had simply dropped his wallet on the way to this woman's house and that was how the lion got it.

The woman had a different surname, and he wondered if she was a married sister, although as he seemed to spend his nights off with her, it might be more natural to assume that she was his fiancée or lover.

Since his wife died, he had found himself reluctant to have a relationship with another woman or even to have sex with one, and he was surprised to find that he felt vaguely jealous of Onda for having a woman to go to on his nights off. He decided to go and visit the woman's apartment, but first he took out a copy of the photograph from Onda's driver's license.

"This is definitely Mr. Onda, isn't it?"

"Yes, no doubt about it, although he isn't bald like that," the concierge said with a frown.

The photograph was not very clear, and Onda had his hair cropped so short that he looked almost bald. Ryosaku looked at it again, but he could not find any similarity between the man in the picture and the memory he had of a five-year-old boy with a soup-bowl haircut.

PART TWO

1 *The Fireman*

The fireman kept worrying about his lost wallet. No matter how hard he tried to forget it, the problem was still lurking at the back of his mind. When could he have lost it? He always kept it in the back pocket of his jeans, and he remembered Chieko once telling him that he should keep it somewhere else as he was asking to have it stolen, walking around with it like that, but of course he had ignored her.

He had replied that he had eyes in the back of his head, and that he would soon realize if someone tried to pick his pocket, but the real reason was that he did not have anywhere else to put it. He knew that it was stupid to keep a wallet there, but what else could he do?

He did not really need to carry his documents at all. He was off duty, and there was no chance of his driving a car on his night off. No, the real reason was probably that he realized that people might think he was acting suspiciously while he was on his patrol, and he wanted his I.D. to prove his authenticity in case he was stopped. Yet, even if he was stopped on his patrols, he still did not need his I.D. All he had to do was to get the police to phone the fire station and they would vouch for him. Perhaps he just felt safer with the documents on him. What if he unconsciously set the fires himself and he was caught in the act? Wouldn't his I.D. or driver's license help act as cover for him?

He knew there was nothing to be gained from thinking this way; it would only drive him crazy. He was the top fireman in his division, so why should he be haunted by fears of being an arsonist?

He decided to go to his girlfriend's apartment. He still had her key. If he was to return it, it would mean the end of their relationship. They would become complete strangers, hating each other, but still filled with a slight feeling of regret.

She was out when he arrived, but he made himself at home, had a shower, and opened a bottle of beer. In the shower, he cursed the low water pressure. They would never be able to put out a fire with the pressure as low as it was. He thought fondly of the writhing hoses he had held in his hands as he fought against fires and wondered if he would ever be able to hold one again.

He woke up to find himself lying on her bed in the nude, with her looking down at him maternally.

"It's terrible, you are in all the newspapers and magazines!" she exclaimed when she saw that he was awake.

"They're all full of lies. I refuse to read any of them." That was not true. He had read all the papers and magazines from cover to cover and wondered if he could really have acted as they said and not have been aware of it.

"That's right. They make it sound as if it is you who is

setting all these fires, but they will catch the real culprit soon and then you will become a hero. I trust you and understand why you make your night patrols."

"But I must admit, I can see why they want to blame me. After all, my I.D. card and license were found in the stomach of a lion that died in a fire. It is hardly surprising that they want to make a fuss about it. I wish now that I had taken your advice and not kept my wallet in my back pocket."

Her sympathy made him feel sorry for himself, and they drew closer together.

"But how could the lion have eaten your wallet? Do you remember dropping it?"

"No, not at all. I left feeling upset after that stupid row we had, and it was not as if I had any money in it, so I didn't pay it much attention. I didn't need to carry it to begin with. I must have been mad."

He hit himself on the head to demonstrate just how stupid he was, but Chieko walked over and hugged his head to her breasts. He had lost his mother at the age of three, and found that, sitting there with his head cradled between a woman's breasts, he was filled with a sense of well-being, which he had not known since childhood.

"The magazines are saying all kinds of things about you. They say that you had been drinking with that woman in her house and that you had sex together."

"The people who write that kind of thing must be mad. I merely asked her politely to clear away the cardboard boxes that she had piled outside her front door, and for some reason she suddenly lost her temper."

Things could very easily have happened as the magazines

said. He could have gone up to her room, and after having a whiskey on the rocks with her, they could have had sex together. If that had happened, there might never have been a fire. No, he must not think like that. If he had gone up to her room, the fire would have happened just the same, and his remains would have been found in the wreckage together with those of the woman and her lion. That at least would have provided incontrovertible proof of his innocence.

He hit his head again.

"But what if I am the arsonist? What if I go around lighting fires without even realizing it? We've all heard of people with dual personalities!"

"But you are not like that," the girl said, hugging his head to her. He realized that she must be a very good nurse. "But if you did not go into her room, how did your documents get there?"

"I suppose I may have dropped them. I had bent down to pick up the boxes, but she soon came out and stopped me."

"But how could they have got into the lion's stomach?"

"I don't know. Perhaps she stole them. She kept saying lewd things to try to annoy me and in the end she even grabbed my crotch. She was drunk and I could see there was nothing to be gained by staying there, so I left. She could easily have reached out and taken my wallet when I turned. That must be it."

"You say that she grabbed your crotch?" the girl asked, watching his face closely.

"Not exactly. She tried to, but I brushed her hand away."

He tried to remember exactly what had happened, but his memory of the occasion was now rather fragmentary, and he could not say for sure what happened at any particular moment.

"So you say that she stole your wallet and then fed it to her pet lion? But if she doted over that animal, why would she want to feed it something like a wallet?"

"How the hell am I supposed to know? For all I know that lion might have had a special weakness for firemen's I.D. cards," he said irritably, but as he spoke he suddenly remembered just how it had been that night. He had half pushed the woman away and then backed off himself. He had kept his back turned away from her, so there was no way that she could have taken the wallet from the back pocket of his jeans.

The woman had not taken his wallet, he was sure of that, but he could not feel so sure that he had not left it on top of the dresser in this room where it was now. He could have left it there when he had stormed out in a temper that night, and Chieko . . . He almost confronted her with his thoughts, but the idea was too terrible even to contemplate.

Still hugging his head to her breast, she lay down on the bed next to his naked body, but he found that he was completely devoid of desire.

2   *The Detective*

Ryosaku sat in the chair in the reception area of the hospital for thirty minutes until the woman he was waiting for emerged. With its rows of seats, the reception hall of the university hospital looked almost like a cinema, and there were about a hundred persons sitting around watching the television while they waited for their names to be called.

He was waiting for the fireman's girl, and when she finally appeared and walked quickly toward the exit, he noticed that she looked completely different in ordinary clothes than when she was wearing her uniform.

He was amazed again at how many coincidences there were in life. It was a coincidence that his wife died in a traffic accident, and it was also a coincidence that the nurse who had tended her through the last week of her life had been the fireman's girl whom he was now following. Even as he sat with his dying wife, he had been attracted to the nurse, and he also felt that her interest in him went beyond mere sympathy. Of course, he had hidden his feelings toward her and remained the devoted husband to the end. After all, he had loved his wife very much, and they had only been married for a year. Still, he could not stifle the feelings of envy he felt toward the fireman.

He followed the nurse to a bookstore near the station where she removed a large medical book from the shelves and studied it earnestly. There were several medical colleges in the area, and as a result the bookstores carried a good selection of medical textbooks.

He stood near her and took down a simple book on home medicine and started to read the chapter on cancer. He was not of an age to get cancer, and he felt that it was pointless to worry about it anyway as he was just as likely to get run down by a car as his wife had been. All the same, he had given up smoking after his wife had died, as he wanted to avoid lung cancer.

The nurse closed her book, and as the detective put his book back on the shelf their eyes met. He gave a start of recognition, and she reciprocated with a confused nod. She had obviously forgotten who he was. After all, it had been two years since his wife's accident.

"Thank you for looking after my wife when she was in the hospital," he said politely.

She frowned slightly as she tried to remember who he was. He had felt very attracted to her, and she had left a strong impression on his mind, but apparently she had not felt quite so moved.

"Oh yes, your wife. I am sorry that we were not able to do more for her, but even now, very few people manage to recover after that operation."

"That's all right. Even if she did recover, she would probably have been bedridden for the rest of her life, so it was probably better that way." He was only trying to make conversation, but the truth was that he really believed what he was saying. "If you're not in a hurry, could we speak together for a short while?"

He felt that he was rushing things a bit, but even if she refused him, he only had to show her his I.D. and put the conversation on an official footing. But she agreed without protest, so it was not necessary. They kept their conversation on a nurse-and-bereaved-husband footing.

"Are you off duty? You seem to be very interested in your work, studying in your spare time like that," he said, referring to the book she had been reading.

"Yes, I heard somewhere that normal people were capable of lighting fires and killing others without being aware of what they were doing, and I wondered what the experts say. Apparently, the subject acts like a sleepwalker, and it is quite possible for him to do things like that and yet remain completely ignorant of what he has done. But I seem to remember that you were connected with the police. What is your opinion?" she asked with a smile.

"Well, it is true that there are people with psychosomatic disorders who are not held responsible for their actions, but . . ."

Whatever the law might say, he found it very difficult to see the difference. There was a case recently where a man had set fire to a bus, killing several people, and although he had been declared innocent due to insanity, Ryosaku could not agree.

"Are there really people with split personalities, though?" he asked with a disarming smile. He managed to make it sound as if his question was quite unconnected to his work.

The nurse hesitated for a moment, then changed the subject to talk about the detective instead.

"Did you remarry?"

"No, I am still single."

"You did not have any children, did you?"

"No, it would have been very hard if I had been left to bring up any children, but as it is, I just reverted to life as a bachelor and do very much as I like."

"It must be pretty rough, though, having to cook all your own meals."

"No, I am used to it now, and anyway I have most of my meals out. The hardest bit is having to eat on my own every day. It would be nice to have someone to talk to sometimes."

"I know what you mean. I feel the same, especially on a day like today when I have just come off the night shift. Even though I feel exhausted and just want to collapse in bed, it would also be nice if there were someone to have a drink and a chat with first."

"I know what you mean."

The detective wondered if he should treat this meeting as a personal one or whether he should stick to business. The way the conversation was going, however, it looked as if it could lead to a meaningful relationship between them. It would be a shame to let the chance slip away.

"Well, let's drink and have a chat then," he said in a cheerful tone, although he felt a bit guilty when he saw the caution fade from her eyes to be replaced with pleasure.

"But what about your work?"

"That's O.K. I only came here to check up on a case of hit-and-run, and that's finished now."

He decided that his investigation of her lover could wait, at least for today. He took her to an old Italian restaurant where he ordered a bottle of Chianti and a bowl of pasta with a spicy marinara sauce. He and his wife had had a similar meal when they were on their honeymoon in San Francisco, and it brought back all kinds of memories.

He spoke of his dead wife and of his theory that everything in the world is governed by chance. As time passed, he found himself growing happier and happier. When the girl told him she had a bottle of wine that a friend had given her and asked him back to her apartment to help her drink it, nothing could have felt more natural. The fact that he would be visiting the room of the lover of the fireman he was investigating was pushed to the corner of his mind.

After they had drunk half of the wine, he had taken a shower and then climbed into her bed, just as the fireman had done earlier. As he did so, he wondered fleetingly what his position would be if it turned out that the fireman was indeed the arsonist.

"You remember that book I was reading about split personalities? Well, I am the same. When I get into bed with a man, I change into another person. But I probably won't even remember you afterward, so never mention it. It would only embarrass me."

She breathed hotly into his ear as she spoke then started to move over his body with her lips and tongue.

3 *The Arsonist*

Michitaro drove his red sports car into the garage of a hotel that was owned by the insurance company his grandfather had founded. He parked the car and walked into the lavatory, where he paused to look at himself in the mirror.

He was a pale, ineffectual-looking man who had obviously led a sheltered childhood. When he was behind the wheel of his sports car, he was a completely different man—quick, decisive, aggressive. But what good would that do him now? He must have been mad to agree to meet the daughter of the Fire Chief. He felt an urge to burst out laughing, but the face in the mirror looked as if it were about to burst into tears.

He walked into the tearoom to one side of the lobby, a large room with a high ceiling, and there, sitting on one of the sofas, were his mother's friend and the young girl she wanted to introduce to him. The older woman was an ex-student of his mother's who delighted in matchmaking. She had managed to bring more than a hundred couples together so far, and it seemed to be all she lived for. To look at her, you might think she was a breeder of champion poodles, looking for new studs. Michitaro felt more like a dog on display than the son of a rich family. There they were, a young man and a young woman, both of good pedigree and good education, who were sure to produce children that would benefit mankind.

The only problem was that he was rotten, he thought, rotten through and through, and no good would come of marrying him. He was different from other people.

The girl had only graduated from music college the year before, and, looking at her graceful fingers, he surprised himself by thinking that a life spent married to her could not be bad. Not that it could ever be, of course, not while his mother was still alive. Also, there was his problem. All the same, he still could not believe that someone would try to marry him off to the daughter of the Fire Chief. It would be funny if it was not so tragic.

"I never realized how grown up you had become, Michitaro!" the older woman said in an exaggerated tone. "But don't mind me. I am only here to introduce you two. Don't hesitate to say if you think that you will not be able to get on. Nobody is going to force you to get married, but remember, first impressions are the most important."

It was obvious that she was used to this kind of thing and was trying to put them both at ease.

"Anyone would think that she was trying to put us off!" Michitaro said brightly after she had left them alone.

"Don't worry about it. She is always like that. I have been through this several times with her already."

She answered him cheerfully. It was obvious that both

of them had come here without the least intention of getting married.

"What kind of people did she introduce you to before?"

"Oh, they would all have made perfect husbands. I was the one who did not make the grade."

"You're joking."

"No, it's true."

"I find that very hard to believe. You must have made up some story to scare them off."

"That's right. I tell them that I turn into a monster at night and lap the oil out of the lamps like they do in the ghost stories."

"You don't fool me," he replied, laughing. Despite all his reservations, they were getting on really well. "Nobody has oil lamps these days."

"That's a point. Maybe I should say that I drink the kerosene out of the stove."

"Yes, that would probably do it, but rather you than me. I wouldn't fancy having to get by on a diet of kerosene."

"No, I suppose your mother feeds you a better diet than that."

He had to admire the way she brought the conversation around to his home life. The fact that she was interested must mean that she was attracted to him a little.

"Oh, my mother is a great believer in freedom of choice. She says I should eat anything my body demands. She says she does not want to live too close to me after I get married and that she will not interfere with my daily life. As long as she can come around once a year or so and have a meal with the family, she will be happy."

"She's just saying that. After all, there are only the two

of you, and I am sure that she will not let you go that easily."

"No, I think that she really means it. But nobody wants to believe her. They think that because I am an only son she will want to keep me tied to her apron strings forever." He sounded a bit uncomfortable.

"I'm sorry, I did not mean it like that. It is just that when I was in high school, I read the book she published of your correspondence with her, and I was very moved by it. I remember thinking that if I could have a son like that, I would not need to have a lover."

He blushed when she mentioned the letters he had written to his mother. She told him of her impression that he was a lover of sorts, and she had been right on target; his letters had in fact been love letters. He had always felt his mother's presence behind him, and even now, it felt as if she were there, urging him on.

"That's silly, it's like saying that just because you are the daughter of a fire chief, you would know how to put out a fire. Now tell me, if the oil in the pan caught fire when you were frying and spread to the curtains, would you put out the curtains first or the oil in the pan?"

"If I had a fire extinguisher, I would put out the fire in the pan first and then turn off the gas. Is that the right answer? You know, my father is a very methodical man and turns the gas off at the main every night, whereas my mother is a bit absentminded, but they seem to get on very well. By the way, to get back to our talk of drinking kerosene, did you know that I am very sensitive to the smell of gasoline? My friends say that when it comes to gasoline, my sense of smell is as keen as a dog's."

She laughed gaily, but Michitaro could not understand why she should have brought up the subject. His face had frozen in shock when she first said it, and he had hurriedly picked up his teacup to hide behind. But she did not appear to have meant anything in particular by it, and he managed to calm himself down again.

"You must take after your father. You would probably be good at putting out fires, too. Maybe you should marry a fireman."

He spoke coldly, but he meant it. It would be taking a joke too far if the daughter of the Fire Chief were to marry an arsonist.

"My father seemed to think the same thing and he has already introduced me to someone whom he thought would be suitable."

"Didn't you hit it off with him?"

"Well, you know how it is . . ." She paused for a moment, then seemed to make up her mind. "It was that fireman they're making all that fuss about in the papers these days. You know, the one whose I.D. card was found in the stomach of the lion that died in a fire."

"Oh, you mean the one who spends his nights off patrolling the streets? I wouldn't be surprised if he turned out to be the arsonist. You never can tell," he said spitefully.

"I don't know. He did not strike me as being that type. He was, how would you say it, . . . he seemed like a man with a mission. He knew just what he wanted to do and was going to do it regardless."

"To hear you defend him like that, am I to take it that you liked him?"

"No, my mother has told me what it is like to be married

to a man in a dangerous job, and I don't think that I am strong enough to stand the tension."

"But human beings soon adjust to any kind of strain or tension," Michitaro said, but then he realized that he was giving away too much about himself, which could be dangerous, so he soon changed the subject.

"If you want to know what kind of man I really am, you'll have to come for a ride in my car. As soon as I get behind the wheel, I become a different person altogether," he said, and invited her to a meal in Yokohama's Chinatown.

"You know, I love all kinds of thrills—the roller coasters in the fair, climbing trees, anything; the only thing that scares me is fires," she said in a small voice.

4   *The Fireman*

The hotel bar was dimly lit, and even though it was still mid-afternoon it gave the impression that it was already dusk outside. Ikuo had just come off a long night shift and was sitting at one end of the bar, sipping a bourbon and soda. He was feeling a little groggy from lack of sleep, and he found the atmosphere in the bar conducive to the way he felt. He was waiting for a reporter from a weekly magazine, and when the other arrived he saw that it was a man a few years older than himself who would soon turn forty.

"You are in a very difficult position, Mr. Onda."

The reporter was obviously worried about getting drunk that early in the afternoon and ordered a tomato juice with just a dash of vodka in it.

"Yes, I know, I've heard it all before. People say that it

is strange that I should try to catch the arsonist on my own. They say I should leave that to the police and just concentrate on putting out fires."

"Yes, but the fire brigade is also responsible for fire prevention, and after all, that is what you were doing, wasn't it? You were trying to prevent arson, not to capture the arsonist, weren't you?"

The reporter wanted the fireman to understand that he was on his side from the beginning.

"Let's be honest. You would like to catch him, wouldn't you? I feel the same," he said flatteringly.

"No, I did not want to capture him. I just wanted to prevent the fire before it started." He sounded annoyed and gulped down half his drink, although it was mostly himself that he was annoyed with.

"But how can you do that if you don't know who the arsonist is?"

"I don't know who he is, but I know how he works. I know how he thinks."

The fireman lifted his glass to eye level and watched the bubbles as they rose to the surface. He wondered why he should know so much about the arsonist's techniques—almost as if they were his own. Suddenly he wished he could crush the glass in his hands.

"And how does he think?" the reporter asked in a small voice, leaning forward.

"I think that he has the soul of a poet." He realized all of a sudden that he had read this in a book on psychology, but it summed up exactly the way he felt the other man behaved. The reporter remained silent.

"Did you ever read the story of the little match girl by

Hans Christian Andersen? You must have read it as a child."

He could still visualize the book's illustration of a little girl with brown hair and long eyelashes. She had been standing in the snow, shielding the flame of a match from the wind, and at her feet was a pile of dead matches.

"The girl had been told to sell the matches, but finally she became so cold and hungry that she lit one to warm her hands. In the center of the flame, she saw a cheerful fire and a large table with a white cloth, piled high with a huge feast. . . ."

He broke off. In his mind's eye, the vision of the match girl became confused with that of Chieko naked in bed with him.

"What has the match girl got to do with this present case?"

"Like the girl in the story, he always uses a whole box of matches. I don't know what he sees in the flame, but he always strikes a whole box of matches and leaves them scattered at his feet."

"Why do you think he does that? It must be very dangerous for him to do so. You would think he would want to light the fire with his first match and then get away as fast as he could."

"Exactly. The most dangerous thing for him is to be seen by someone while he is actually lighting the fire. Like any other crime, the worst thing would be for him to be caught in the act."

"And that is why you say he is a poetic man?"

"No, not quite. You see, from what we can tell of his actions, the act of striking the matches is even more important to him than escaping. He always uses a whole box of matches, and I feel that he must see some kind of a vision in the flames as he strikes them one after the other, just like the little match girl."

As he spoke, the fireman felt a load come off his chest, but whether this was the result of discussing his theory with another man or just the bourbon spreading through his system, he could not be sure.

"Maybe he is just a careful man, and he strikes a whole box of matches just to make sure that the fire catches," the reporter said, but even he did not sound very convinced.

"No. The match ends are all found in one place. The only thing that could explain it would be if he stood there lighting one match after another and letting them fall to the ground."

"That's a bit strange."

"That's why I said there was something of the poet in him. I think it would be a mistake just to say he is mad. There is something about his actions that can't be explained away so easily. Sometimes I feel that I can almost sympathize with him. I did not realize it at first, but I feel something."

"I know what you mean. It does strike a chord, doesn't it?"

The reporter and the fireman felt a bond form between them and raised their glasses to each other.

"Does he have any other characteristics?"

"Yes, cardboard boxes. He will never set fire to anything else, just cardboard boxes. They seem to excite him."

"You mean like catnip to a cat?" the reporter asked.

"No, it goes beyond that. I think they are an essential part of his life."

"So you think that in order to capture him we should

study him and learn his habits, as if he were a wild animal we were hunting?"

"Well, at least I think we have to analyze his methods, although it is no good to think about it logically. We have to try to think like him."

"With the spirit of a poet?"

The reporter had substituted spirit for soul, but Ikuo did not bother to correct him.

"But this puts you in a difficult, if not dangerous, position. Surely, as you have found out this much about the arsonist's methods, the answer is quite simple. All you have to do is to make sure that there are no cardboard boxes left out where he can see them."

"Yes, that is why I conduct my midnight patrols."

"In that case, surely the second part of your plan would be to leave some boxes somewhere that he could find them, and then catch him when he sets fire to them."

The fireman remained silent.

"Are you sure you haven't tried to catch him already? Wasn't that fire in which the woman with the pet lion died your trap?"

"No!"

He jumped to his feet, but even as he did so, he felt the certainty creep over him that those boxes had indeed been left outside the woman's house in order to attract the arsonist.

"There is no need to get upset. All the other magazines are saying that you are the arsonist, but I think that idea is too hackneyed for words. A fireman setting fires in his spare time. It sounds more like a cartoon story than a news

57

story. It just doesn't seem to fit. I don't think that you did it, but the police have decided to investigate you, and you are being kept under surveillance, you know."

The fireman was hardly even listening to him. *If those boxes outside the house of the woman with the lion had really been left there to lure the arsonist . . .*

Despite the fact that he had just finished his drink, he felt his mouth suddenly become dry.

5   *The Detective*

The detective stopped for an early dinner with his partner in a restaurant at the top of Bandit's Hill. His partner was a younger man than he and still a bachelor. The detective remembered his old partner with affection. He had been a much older man who had retired recently, and although they had sometimes gotten on each other's nerves, he had trained Ryosaku well, and Ryosaku missed him now that he was gone. His new partner was still in his twenties, and although Ryosaku was only in his early thirties himself, working with him made him feel very old.

"Our man has just come off duty, so I think we can expect him to sleep for some time," the younger man said. "He took in all the papers that had been delivered while he was on duty, went to the local supermarket to buy some frozen noodles, then returned home. He had a bath, ate the noodles, looked through the paper, and then I think he went to bed. The light was soon extinguished."

"We can't be sure that he has gone to bed, though. I bet that you sometimes go and visit a massage parlor after you have been on duty without going to bed first."

"Who, me? It is true that still being young, I can go for two or three nights without sleep, but I never have to pay for it, not like some old men! But seriously, don't you think the reason he went straight to bed like that might be to get ready for his night patrols?"

"I don't know. He never goes out these days. I think that he has stopped doing it."

"I wonder why. Do you think that he has caught wind of us?"

The younger man did not seem to be very worried, and Ryosaku realized that as soon as he went off duty he would forget all about their fireman. He would probably be off to some girl's bed or a disco or something. It was only natural at that age. After a few moment's thought, Ryosaku picked up the bill.

"I want to stay here and think a while before I go back to work. I doubt that our man has gone out again."

"O.K. Well, thanks for the meal," the young man said and walked out of the restaurant with a wave.

Ryosaku wondered why he had offered to pay for his partner's dinner, and he decided that it was probably in an effort to convince himself that he was satisfied with the way the younger man was doing his job.

A short while later he left the restaurant and walked down the gentle Gonnosuke Hill. When he reached the Meguro River, he headed back up Bandit's Hill again. As he walked, he thought about the humpbacked bridge that had stood over the river two centuries before, and about the bandits who had lurked there. Compared with the crimes he had to deal with, banditry was a very crude and simple crime, and he wondered when it was that people had started to apply their intellect to crime. He realized that intellect was probably not the ideal word, but it was the best he could think of. As society became more complicated, so did the crimes, or at least they were not always as straightforward as they appeared to be.

He was feeling much more positive after his meal as he pushed open the side door to the Kaenji Temple. The light from a nearby construction site lit the temple grounds, and the small stone Buddhas stood out in the night like some kind of modern art. He was not a religious man, and if the construction of the condominiums around the temple was responsible for the destruction of the small statues, he would not be particularly upset. The apartments were necessary for the people who were alive now, and he had no sympathy for the environmentalists who were protesting the construction.

He was not interested in the statues that had been erected in memory of the people who had died in fires during the feudal period, rather, he had come to see the small statue of an animal. He walked through the hundred statues until he found it again, out of sight at the back, a small stone animal with a mane like a lion. Having checked that it was still there, he made his way toward the priests' quarters.

A protest meeting against the construction of the condominiums was just coming to an end, and he was met by a young priest who introduced himself as the head priest's representative. Despite his shaved head and priest's robes, the young man did not seem to have committed himself to spiritual matters and appeared to be more worried about the redevelopment of the area, which could damage the stone Buddhas.

"I am here to ask about the statue of a lion you have on your grounds."

He showed his identification to make it clear that he was here as part of an official investigation, but even he could not tell if this was true or whether he was doing it for personal reasons.

"A lion? I know nothing about any lion. Now if you will excuse me, we are very busy. We have to protect the cultural assets in our care."

The priest spoke bluntly and tried to look annoyed, but it was obvious that he was worried by the question.

"Well, it may not be a lion. I suppose it could be a dog." As he spoke, he suddenly realized that it probably was a dog. But he also realized that if it were not a lion it could have no connection to the fire. If that were true, how could he explain his presence in the temple?

Ryosaku felt the eyes of the departing protesters on him as the priest led him to the main hall of the temple and indicated that they should sit down in front of the main Buddha there. They sat down in silence for a few moments while the young priest calmed down and gathered his thoughts.

"This is a problem of faith. No new statues are permitted to be erected on the temple grounds as they would not be classified as cultural treasures, and we have to protect the temple's heritage above everything else. Do you understand?"

Ryosaku remained silent. He was remembering a time

61

in his childhood when he had been led to a new statue in these temple grounds and urged to admit what he had done.

"However, there are people who love their pets as if they were children. In fact, they believe that they are reincarnations of children who died in traffic accidents, and when the pet dies they beg us to allow them to place an image of the pet in amongst the statues of Buddha. They are so ardent in their requests that I feel forced to turn a blind eye, although the chief priest knows nothing about it, and we cannot condone it openly."

Ryosaku wished that the priest had not said that the dog was a reincarnation of a child that had died in a traffic accident, as traffic accidents held special connotations for him, and he found the idea of the unborn child in his wife's womb being reincarnated as a dog repugnant.

"I don't suppose you could tell me who put that statue there, could you? Of course we will keep their name confidential and won't even let it be known that the statue exists. I presume from the fact that the statue is placed where it is that the pet in question died in a fire. Could you tell me when it was?"

The priest looked anguished and wiped his forehead with a handkerchief. Ryosaku suddenly realized that the young priest must have pocketed the money he received for permitting the statue to be erected there without telling the chief priest.

"As you know, like lawyers we are obliged to keep our client's business secret, and I don't think that I would be permitted to divulge the name to you."

"Am I to understand that the dog died in connection

with a crime? But anyway, what kind of dog is it? A Japanese dog? A German shepherd?"

"Well, actually I heard that it was a lion," the priest said with a sigh.

"But when I asked, you said that it wasn't a lion."

"I know, but you obviously came here thinking that it was connected to the lion that died in the fire recently. But that statue was put there at least one month before the fire, so, you see, there cannot be any connection between the two."

He wiped his brow again.

"Excuse me for asking, but how much money did the person who erected the statue leave as an offering?"

"They did not leave an offering as such, but they are also worried about what would happen to the other statues if the condominiums are permitted to be built, and they gave a substantial donation to help us in our fight against their construction. They particularly requested me not to let their name be known, and I feel obliged to respect their wishes."

Ryosaku stood up and walked toward the door. As he was about to leave, he turned.

"Was it a man or woman?" he asked.

The priest sat staring at the floor, shaking his head slowly from side to side. Gone was the militant protester, and in his place was a man who knew his own weaknesses all too well.

6   *The Arsonist*

With a hangover, Michitaro sat down to his breakfast of whole wheat toast and yogurt. He forced himself to eat, as he knew that if he did not his mother would become cross with him again. She firmly believed that the toast and yogurt were vital for his well-being, and she would not take any excuses if he did not have an appetite.

"How was the girl yesterday? Tell me about her. I'm interested in how it went."

He knew that she would have had a full report of everything that happened, but he went along with her playacting anyway.

"She was a terrific girl. I would say that she is ninety-nine percent perfect for me, only . . ."

He knew that it was dangerous to bait his mother like this, but life with her would be unbearable if he could not taunt her just a little. Sure enough, she could not resist.

"Only what? What was the one percent that you did not like?"

"Her father's profession. I don't like the fact that he is the Fire Chief."

"Why on earth not? Would it be better if he was the Chief of Police?"

His mother stood and watched him without changing her expression. He knew that he would not be able to stand the tension for long, but he did not dare push his luck any further. He wanted to say that the Chief of Police would be all right, that it would be too ridiculous for an arsonist to marry the daughter of the Fire Chief, but instead, he merely ate the last piece of toast and answered that the Chief of Police would be the same.

"I would have to be careful how I acted if I married the daughter of a public figure like that."

"Aren't you being a bit prejudiced? They say that her

father is an easygoing man. Why don't you like him being the Fire Chief?"

His mother seemed determined to get an answer. She had told him that it was entirely up to him if he wanted to get married to that girl, but it would appear that she had gone to a lot of trouble to check up on her. He knew that she never hesitated to employ a detective when she thought that it was necessary, and he had seen an advertisement for one lying by the telephone recently.

"I don't have any real reason . . ."

"Are you still worrying about what happened when you were a boy? That was more than twenty years ago. You were still in kindergarten, so there is no reason to worry that anyone will bring it up now. Anyway, it wasn't you who started that fire. That much I know."

His mother closed her eyes, and an expression of pain and distress crossed her face. He regretted having started this, as his real aim was to avoid causing her pain.

"Those other two children you were playing with that day have already forgotten all about what happened."

"I have forgotten, too, or rather, I am no longer very clear about the details." He chose his words carefully. "It's just that even now, when I hear a fire engine's siren my heart sinks. I wish they could do something about the sound of the fire engine siren, make it gentler like that of a police car," he said, changing the subject.

Giving him a searching look, his mother replied, "But there are lots of people who feel relieved to hear that sound—people who are waiting to be rescued. Although there are also some sick people who find that the sound gives them a thrill."

She said this last in a sarcastic lilt. Not to be outdone, he had one last try.

"Yes, but I still don't think I will be able to marry the Fire Chief's daughter . . ." He suddenly thought up a great excuse, and his eyes sparkled with excitement. His mother gave him a searching look.

"When I hear the sound of a siren, it makes me impotent. There would be no point in my getting married if we weren't able to have children, would there?"

He stood up and walked through to the next room, where a poodle puppy was sleeping.

"If dogs have an I.Q., this one's must be very high. He's sure to become a champion. Not only does he look very good, but he's clever, too, although that's only to be expected with his pedigree."

He had hoped to change the subject, but he realized his mistake when his mother followed him into the room.

"Please don't set fire to him like you did the last one. I sometimes think that there must be something wrong with you to set fire to your pet dog like that."

"I didn't do it on purpose. I told you, he got some white paint on him, and when I tried to get it off with benzene he ran away and went too near the stove. He did it himself. It was not me."

"Your dog was too clever to do something like that. You must have been trying to teach him some strange tricks again."

So she did suspect him after all! She had not said anything at the time.

"Don't worry, it was an accident. It won't happen again."

66

He was about to add that even a lion had died in a fire, but he kept silent.

"Well, anyway, please be careful. Last time it happened in the basement, so the fire didn't spread, but you may not be so lucky next time. If we were to have another fire, people would talk."

He remained silent.

When his mother had asked where he had taken the girl for a meal the night before, he just said Yokohama. He did not mention that he had taken her to a Chinese restaurant there, as his doctor had warned him to avoid a high-calorie diet. He had refrained from mentioning this fact to the girl, too.

PART
THREE

1 *The Detective*

The detective sat down on a bench in the park and looked at the fountain, which was out of action for repairs.

"Stick to that fireman for all you are worth." He repeated the Chief Inspector's words to himself in a low voice. Normally he would have thought nothing of it, but this time he felt the words had some special meaning.

Ikuo Onda. The name echoed in his memory, but he still could not put his finger on it. He wondered if it wasn't just that girl. He should never have allowed himself to become involved with her, but she was the first woman who had interested him since his wife died. Of course, the sex had been great, but that was not all. There was something else about her that appealed to him.

He saw her walking toward him and stood up from the bench. She even walked like a nurse, he noticed—brisk, efficient, and with a sense of purpose.

"Now I know why you are interested in me. You have been investigating me, haven't you?"

She stood in front of him with her hands on her hips, and he sat back down on the bench.

"The ward sister told me that the police have been asking about my duty roster and checking up on my records, but it's not me you're interested in, is it? It's Ikuo Onda."

It was the first time she had mentioned the fireman by name. Ryosaku shook his head slowly from side to side while he tried to think what to say.

"You're wrong. It's because you looked after my wife."

Her expression softened a little.

"But you must know that I am Ikuo's girl. Do you think the fact that Ikuo was in my room on the night the lion died has some special meaning?"

"Everyone is interested in that case, but you must realize that we have any number of other cases to keep us busy."

He felt a pang of conscience at hiding his true intentions from her. He wondered why he bothered. Would it impede his investigations, or was it simply that he secretly hoped that what had started between them the other day might blossom into something important?

"Why did you call and ask to see me after I finish my work? Did you want me to sit with you in the park like this as if we were lovers? Don't you know that I already have a lover? He spends his nights off with me in my bed, and we have sex together. After that he always goes out alone, and on those nights there is always a fire."

She sat on the bench next to Ryosaku, and, putting her face in her hands, she started to sob.

"Did he go out on the night that the woman with the lion died?"

"Yes. We were both satisfied after having sex, but then he suddenly put on his jeans and went out. He's mad!"

"Do you mean to say that you think he is the arsonist? Even though he is a fireman?"

"Yes, but I read somewhere that arsonists are driven by frustration, so why does he only do it after he has had sex with me?"

"I don't know, but they also say that it is a kind of exhibitionism."

Ryosaku stirred the sand below the bench with the toe of his shoe. He could see that she loved the fireman very much, and he involuntarily pictured the two of them in bed together. If that was the case, however, why had she invited him back to her room the other night? Had it been the alcohol or was it just that he had been around when she had needed a man?

"I have not seen him since that night. We had a fight, and I think he's trying to avoid me. Maybe he realized that I knew he was the arsonist."

"But there have not been any fires since then." He wondered if this was a good thing or not. "Next time he says he wants to see you, I would appreciate it if you could let me know."

"Why? Do you want to come and watch us in bed together? I am sorry, I did not mean that. I don't know what's wrong with me recently. I have the reputation for being a good nurse, but as soon as I get off duty, I just don't know what to do. I think I am heading for a nervous breakdown. Yes, I'll get in touch. If he says he wants to see me, I'll call the police station. O.K.?"

She put her hands together on her lap, and Ryosaku felt the urge to hold them.

"I thought I would invite you to the movies today, but you look tired."

"Yes, it was all I could do to make it over here, but I felt that I had to tell you what I knew about Ikuo."

So saying, she stood up and walked away from him in her brisk nurse's walk. She did not look back at him once, and he suddenly felt very empty. He had planned to take her out to the movies, to a restaurant, then back to her apartment for some more sex. After they finished, he had hoped to bring the subject around to Ikuo Onda, but she had put an end to all of that.

All the same, why had the Chief Inspector checked up on her without saying anything to him? Why had he checked on the duty hours of the fireman's girl? This was not the way things were usually done.

Sitting there on the bench, he forced himself to think about his role in the investigation and about the file that the Chief Inspector had given to him on the woman who had kept the lion.

The woman had worked in a foreign circus until three years ago, and the lion she kept was not just a normal lion, but a trained circus lion. Why had the Inspector given the file directly to him without going through the usual chain of command? And the fireman's I.D.—how had that gotten into the stomach of the lion?

His thoughts returned to the statue of the lion at the temple, and he decided to go there again. The way he felt at the moment, he would prefer to be with statues than with real people.

2   *The Fireman*

Ikuo could feel someone watching him. It had been like that for some time now, but whenever he looked around, there was nobody to be seen. At first he had thought that it was all his imagination, but now he was convinced that he was being kept under surveillance by the detectives who were investigating the arson case, and, strangely enough, this made him feel a lot better. It awoke a defiant streak in him. After all, he could not be the arsonist. He was the man who had been hunting the arsonist for so long.

He was very upset after breaking up with Chieko, and he went to visit a bar in the Setagaya district to cheer himself up. There was a young girl working there who was aspiring to become an actress.

He walked in and ordered the stew that was the specialty there and a glass of cheap whiskey cut with hot water. He was drinking more these days and was aware that it was a bad sign.

One of the regular customers was questioning the long-haired girl who was serving behind the counter. "And then what happened? Is it true what they said in the weeklies? Did you really put your hand in the lion's mouth?"

"Not just my hand, I put my whole head in. It was a very well-trained lion, and it was really cute. I can't bear to think that it died in a fire like that, and I will never forgive that arsonist, whoever he is. After all, I could very well have stayed there that night and been burned to death, too. It was only because I was making a TV appearance the next day that I went home to get my clothes together. I couldn't very well appear in the clothes I had worn to help her move, could I?"

The girl chatted away happily. It was obvious that she had said the same thing numerous times before, but she was not one to complain. She had achieved fame at last and was determined to enjoy it as long as it lasted.

Ikuo sat listening to her, turning has glass in his hands. He had read her story in one of the magazines, and he wondered why, if she had been there, she had not come out to stop that drunken woman when she was shouting at him.

"Where did you meet that woman with the lion?" asked another customer, a young salesman by the look of him, who spoke in a voice thick with alcohol. This was the very question that Ikuo had wanted to ask.

"She was going to appear in a series on TV with me, with her lion, of course. She was a very nice woman and we soon became friends. I had to put my head in her lion's mouth, and it was a good way for me to become friendly with it, too."

"You seem to be very keen on your work," one of the customers said.

"Of course. I have to think about my parts all the time. But you know, that lion had a huge insurance policy taken out on it. They said that if it attacked me on the set, I was just to sit back and let it eat me. It was much more valuable than a mere actress!"

She had obviously made this joke to good effect several times before, and she gave Ikuo a puzzled stare when she noticed that he did not join in the general laughter.

It was the first he had heard of an insurance policy on

the lion. There had not been any mention of it in the weekly magazines or at the meeting at the fire station.

So the lion had been insured, had it? he thought. *I bet the insurance company is regretting it now.*

He did not sympathize with insurance companies very much. Being a fireman, he was considered a high risk and had to pay high rates as a result, but the way he looked at it, the companies made enough money without charging extra to public servants. Anyway, they had obviously considered the lion a better risk than he, and now they would have to pay for their mistake.

He finished his drink and stood up. It was already eleven o'clock, and if he drank any more, he would only get drunk. If that happened, he knew that he would make his way back to his girl's room and then the same thing might happen again. A small flame might blossom and grow to fill the night.

He paid his bill, and as he was leaving, he heard the young actress speak.

"I must go now. If I don't hurry, I will miss the train," she said in a bright voice.

He made his way toward the station and soon heard the sound of footsteps hurrying up from behind.

"Wait a minute, I want to speak to you. You're the fireman who came that night and whose I.D. was found in the lion's stomach, aren't you?"

"Yes. How did you know?"

"I recognized you from the pictures in the magazines. I thought you would come to see me sooner or later, and I wanted to apologize."

75

"Why?"

She took his arm and she sounded a bit winded, so he slowed his pace.

"Because of what I said to the police. I said that you tried to force Mitsuko to tidy up those cardboard boxes, but she was so abusive toward you that you probably came back later and set fire to them. I didn't mean anything by it. It just came out. But it was not you. You don't look the type that goes around setting fire to people's homes . . . or was it you?"

She suddenly looked worried and studied his face closely.

"If it was me, what would you do about it?"

"I would tell you to go and give yourself up to the police. Mitsuko's spirit will never forgive you, nor the lion's either. She told me that the lion was a reincarnation of Napoleon, you know."

"Well, I'm sorry to say that it was not me who set fire to those boxes. But if you were in the house when I was there, why didn't you come down and stop her when she started having a go at me like that?"

"Of course I was there, but I didn't have any clothes on at the time. I had just gotten out of the bath."

She blushed slightly.

"In that case, it cannot be helped. But I thought that if you had come down and helped me clear up the boxes, that fire might never have happened, and your friend and her lion would still be alive today."

"That would have been impossible," she said, dropping her voice. "She would never have let anyone move the stack of cardboard. She said he would never be able to resist a pile of boxes like that, and she said he would come and flap

his wings and breathe fire out of his mouth. I have no idea
what she was talking about. She was really drunk at the
time. You know, she was so drunk that she bit me hard on
the thigh, and I still have the mark to prove it."

He wondered if she was a bit simple, telling things like
that to a complete stranger.

"Did you tell the police what you just told me?"

"No, I would never tell anyone else. I just told you
because I felt that I owed it to you after what I had done.
You see, I thought that if I pretended that I knew who the
arsonist was, I would be able to get my picture in the papers
and appear on the television, which would be good for my
career. I hope you understand."

"Yes, I understand."

He spat out the words and shook her off his arm.

"The garbage men said they would take those boxes away,
but she told them to leave them. She was waiting for someone to come and set fire to them. Don't leave me, please,
don't leave me alone. I am terrified. You can sleep with me
if you like, but just don't leave me alone."

She begged him desperately, but he merely increased
his pace.

So she had left those boxes there as a trap for the arsonist,
just as he had planned to do himself. But if that was the
case, why had she died in the fire?

3   *The Arsonist*

A young clerk brought some documents to Michitaro's desk,
blushing slightly with admiration and yearning as she put

them in his hand. He felt a flush of superiority.

Not everyone in the company could look at the policy that she brought him, but he was in an exalted position. His university, his guarantor, his sponsor, his mother's social position, and the fact that he scored high marks in the entrance examination—all these factors helped him to get where he was now. But above all else was the fact that his grandfather had started the company. In the normal course of events, he would inherit the majority of the company's shares, and everyone knew that it was only a matter of time before he was nominated president.

Sometimes he noticed the present head of the company, an ex–civil servant, looking at him with a mixture of dislike and sympathy, but he wondered what the other would say if he knew that the mere smell of gasoline would make him tremble with ecstasy as he struck the match. He knew that it was only a matter of time before everyone would know what kind of man he was, but in the meantime he just had to do his job and pretend that everything was fine.

He looked at the policy on the lion. It had been insured for an unbelievable amount of money, and the sum would have been more appropriate for a small jet plane than an animal.

The reason why the insurance company had agreed to take out such an excessive policy was that it was limited to the period during which the lion was used in the filming of a TV program, a matter of a few days, and the sole beneficiary was to be its owner. If she also died with the lion, the money was not to be paid to her heirs. Michitaro could not understand why she had agreed to have this clause written into the policy. As she had died with the lion, it meant that the policy was now void. Nobody outside the company would ever get to hear about it. Something had gone wrong with his plans. It was nobody's fault, just a little thing, but everything had been put out of joint.

Michitaro sat and looked at her name on the document. There had only been a few years' difference in their ages, but as she had been married to a foreigner, her surname was not Japanese. She had written the name in an elegant hand, and he noticed that her first name was the same as the famous perfume, Mitsuko.

Her husband, Pierre, had been the illegitimate son of an Oriental father and a French mother. He had worked as a trapeze artist in a circus, but he had died a few years earlier when he fell during his act. His wife had been able to collect on several insurance policies as well as a government policy, so she was very well off, and had lived with her pet lion in a suite in a first-class hotel in the Caribbean. He could not understand why she thought it necessary to take out a policy on the lion that she treated like an only child in order to defraud his company or, for that matter, why the company had agreed to the policy.

The company had been expanding in recent years, and the policy in question had been issued by the New York branch office. He could only guess why they had agreed to it, but he supposed that they wanted to demonstrate to the world just how generous they could be and hoped to use it as P.R. That would explain everything. They probably did not want Mitsuko to die in the fire. They would have been happy to pay the money for the lion as it would have been worth it in advertising value.

Had he known that someone would die when he had set

fire to the boxes? There was only a fifty- or sixty-percent chance, but even so, when had he reached the point where he was willing to let people die in order to satisfy his desires?

If the people in New York knew that it was he who was responsible for the deaths in the fires, they would certainly be surprised. He thought about his grandmother, who was the major shareholder in the company, and when he considered what the shock of such news might do to her, he brightened up considerably.

He realized that he must stop now, and that if he did nobody would ever suspect him. He had never made a mistake. Although his actions had been bold, he had paid full attention to detail, and everything had gone according to plan. Being who he was, he had a good protective camouflage, and, anyway, everybody's attention had been distracted by that clown of a fireman who had blundered onto the scene.

He had read that the fireman had graduated at the top of his class from the fire academy, but he should have just stuck to his hoses instead of playing policeman in his spare time. Who did he think he was, making private patrols in the middle of the night in order to catch the arsonist?

Michitaro felt extremely hostile toward the fireman. He thought of the picture he had seen in the magazine, a strong, resolute face that seemed to strike a chord in his memory, but for the moment he did not connect it with the Ikuo he had known as a child.

The fool had brought it all on himself, trespassing on his preserve like that, and he deserved to become a laughing-stock. Maybe he had wanted to set fire to the boxes himself?

He always worried that someone else might beat him to it, and that night he had had a strong premonition that someone else wanted to set fire to those boxes before he got there. At least he had won that night. He had set fire to the boxes before anyone else.

He felt a strong glow of satisfaction, but it was going to be the last. He had been lucky until now. It was as if the gods were watching over him, but that was only to be expected. He did not light the fires for his own satisfaction. He had done it for the best motives in the world.

But now was the time to stop, he told himself again. He had decided that he was going to marry the Fire Chief's daughter. She was intelligent and attractive, and the mere fact that her father was who he was would act as camouflage for him.

But something bothered him. Why should the New York office have agreed to the policy on the lion? The woman had already received a large payment on her husband's policy, so they should have been suspicious of her from the beginning.

When he thought about it, uncertainty spread through him completely.

4   *The Detective*

The detective walked through the gateway to the Temple of the Flames and noticed that the plum blossoms, which had been in full bloom last time, had already dropped, while the buds on the cherry trees were almost ready to burst open. Although the seasons might change, he found that no matter how hard he tried to drive all thought of Chieko from his mind, he could not forget her.

He had toyed with the idea of giving up the case, but that would not be necessary. For once, fate was offering him an opportunity, and it would be foolish to throw it away. It was mere chance that had allowed him to meet the nurse again, as it had been chance that had led his wife to die in a traffic accident and led him to find the statue of the lion in amongst the Buddhas at the temple. This time, however, fate had dealt him a good hand. Maybe it was to balance out all the bad hands he had had in the past. So thinking, he felt much better and more positive.

He had come to the temple today to meet the chief priest, whom he heard had returned from Kyoto. He walked around to the priests' living quarters, where he was met by the chief priest himself. There was no sign of the young priest whom he had seen before. The chief priest was of an age where he no longer had to shave his head to maintain his priestly appearance. The gentle eyes under the shining forehead blinked rapidly as he tried to hide the confusion that Ryosaku's questions caused him.

"Do you mean to say that the police think someone has been up to mischief with our statues?"

"No, I think that whoever it was who placed the statue of a lion among the others was driven by the best of motives."

"I'm sorry. I am afraid I did not notice it myself."

"It is about twenty inches tall and looks brand new. It first appeared at about the same time that lion died in a fire. I'm sure you must have heard about it."

82

He had touched the heart of the matter, but the priest's expression did not change.

"If you say so, I am sure you must be right. Being here every day as I am, one tends to overlook these things."

It was obvious that he did not know anything about the lion, but Ryosaku did not mention his previous conversation with the young priest.

"Do you know about the case of the lion that died?"

"I believe that I did hear something about it, but I try not to become involved in worldly matters like that."

The old priest seemed to indicate by this that he was not interested.

"If someone who was not a regular believer was to make a statue and put it in among the others like that, would it, in your opinion, help the victim's spirit to find rest?"

"We have a saying, you know. You can carve a Buddha, but you can't make the spirit. If you wanted to help the departed, you would have to have it consecrated."

"So you mean that if the person who put the statue there did it for religious reasons, they would have to ask you to consecrate it for them?"

"I don't know. There are all kinds of people in the world, you know, and they all seem to have their own ideas about religion. But, anyway, let's go and see this statue of yours. There are several statues of animals, you know."

Ryosaku led him past the other statues to the very back, but when they got there, he could hardly believe his eyes. The statue was nowhere to be seen! He looked around in case he had the spot wrong, but there was no sign of the little lion.

"Surely you must at least have taken a photograph of it," the priest said.

Ryosaku did not answer, but just pointed to the notice that stood to the rear, then turned and indicated another one to his side, which read as follows:

Photography of these religious monuments is forbidden without prior permission of the temple authorities.

"You only had to ask me," the priest said with a smile.

"I know," said Ryosaku with an answering smile. "But I did not attach very much importance to it. I never for one moment thought that it might disappear."

He spoke with regret as he realized that he had let a golden opportunity slip through his fingers.

"How about this one. This looks like a lion," the priest said encouragingly, pointing at a traditional statue of a temple dog. Ryosaku looked around and saw that there were several statues of animals amongst the Buddhas, and some of them could indeed have been lions.

"No, it was nothing like that. It was a Western-style carving of a lion with a mane, its tail standing up behind it, and its feet planted firmly on the ground. It was brand new, and it stood out easily from the others."

He could still see the statue in his mind's eye, but he was disgusted with himself for not being able to describe it better. He decided to change the subject.

"Do you remember a new statue that was dedicated in this spot about twenty years ago?"

"No, I have only been here fifteen years, so that would have been during my predecessor's time. Nobody has dedicated a statue since I came. It is not very popular these days. Most people seem to prefer to copy the sutras instead. The person who copies the sutra benefits himself, and it is very easy to do. Anyone can do it."

Ryosaku realized that he had no option but to forget the statue and looked over to where there was a sign concerning the copying of sutras. Suddenly he felt like copying a sutra himself. If he was to do so, he might manage to forget about Chieko, even if only for a short while.

"Now that you mention it, I would like to copy a sutra myself, if I may. At least it would mean that my visit was not a complete waste of time."

"Of course. But don't you think it would be better if you were to come again when you were not on duty and you could relax properly?"

Ryosaku ignored the priest's advice and walked into the main hall of the temple where he knelt down and started to copy out one of the shorter sutras. As he did so, his mind went back to the time when he was about five years old and he had knelt like this to practice calligraphy and painting. He could not remember where it had been, but he could vaguely remember the faces of the two boys who had sat on either side of him. That had been a short while before the fire, but who was it who had struck the first match, and who had struck that fateful one in the cupboard?

Michitaro . . . it was Michitaro whose house had been burned down.

He stopped writing for a moment, then stood up and made his way to the priests' quarters again.

"Excuse me, but may I look at the records of all the people who copied sutras here about two months ago? I am interested in the week before and the week after the night the lion died."

The people who copied out the sutras all wrote their names and addresses on them. Ryosaku did not really think he would find anything. It was more an effort to escape from the memories of his childhood than anything else.

He leafed through the sutras, some of them written in a clear hand and others obviously written by people who were not used to using calligraphy brushes. He was about halfway through when he suddenly stopped. There, dated two days after the fire, was a sutra signed by the fireman, Ikuo Onda.

The sutra itself was written very precisely, character by character, but the name was written in such an uncertain fashion that it looked almost as if it had been written with the left hand.

5   The Fireman

Ikuo had not been to bed for over twenty-four hours. Usually, he would come home, glance through the newspapers that had built up in his mail slot, then have a meal of noodles washed down with a glass of saké. After that, he would collapse into bed and sleep like a log, but tonight was different. He changed into his jeans and jogging shoes, his uniform for his night patrols, then went out again.

He had noticed that he was being followed when he left the fire station, but the detective must have been fooled into thinking that he was going straight to bed as usual, as there was no sign of him now. He hailed a taxi and gave the driver the directions the young actress had given him on the phone that afternoon.

"It is a brand-new building," she had said, "and it looks really nice, you know. It backs onto a park with a lake where I can go jogging, which is really good for my figure. Hey, why don't we go jogging together. I always feel lonely jogging at night. I have a secret I want to tell you. I didn't tell you everything the other day about that woman with the lion."

Ikuo had stood by the phone in the fire station listening to the young starlet chatting away, without being able to get a word in edgewise. He wondered again if she were a bit simple.

"Promise me that you will come tonight. You are off duty, aren't you? I checked with one of the other men just now. We will go running, so don't forget to bring your jogging shoes with you, O.K.? It feels really great to make love after you've built up a sweat running. They say it is quite the 'in' thing in the States at the moment and that a child born after such a coupling is more intelligent than the average child."

Thinking back to her slightly eccentric voice on the phone, he found that he could not feel very enthusiastic about going to see her. What he really wanted to do was visit Chieko. He could picture her white body, which had always welcomed him so, lying open-legged in a drugged stupor from the sleeping pills she took. Desire was building up inside him, but he told himself that the starlet would be adequate to gratify him. He would merely think of her as a prostitute. He felt that he would never make love again. He would simply enjoy sex for its own sake, and if a female was willing to offer it without his even asking, the least he could do would be to go jogging with her.

The building that contained the girl's apartment was built to resemble a French palace and was obviously designed to appeal to single women. The rooms were all very small and he did not like it at all, but at least it would be fairly fireproof, not like Chieko's apartment. His thoughts went back to her, and he knew that he would not be able to get her off his mind as long as he kept the key to her room.

He walked through the doorway of the starlet's room and was met by a deep growl. He looked down in surprise and saw a small animal that resembled a lion.

"I bet you were surprised to see that I have got a lion, too," the starlet said as she bent down to pick up a small gray poodle, which had been trimmed to resemble a lion, and held it to her cheek. "He's got a very good pedigree, but I haven't insured him, so he will not die in a fire."

"I bet he must have been expensive," the fireman said as he removed his jogging shoes. His thoughts went back to the woman with the French name, the pile of cardboard boxes, and the lion roaring in its cage.

"I am only just looking after it for a friend," the starlet said. Putting down the dog, she hugged Ikuo to her. "I'm scared. Someone is after me. They want to kill me. That's why I gave up my job at the bar, and I have even refused all the jobs they offer me on television. I have not told anyone this address but you."

"You're exaggerating. No one wants to kill you."

"No, I mean it. It's an international drug ring. Those cardboard boxes are at the root of it. They only looked as

88

if they held that woman's belongings, but really they were used to smuggle drugs into the country."

She seemed to be genuinely scared. She trembled in his arms, but he could not believe her, and it was all he could do to suppress a laugh. For some reason her words did not ring true. They sounded like a part that she had learned for a TV drama.

"You don't believe me, do you? But it's true. The drugs hidden in those boxes were worth a fortune."

"You can't expect me to believe that. If they were so valuable, why would she leave them lying in the street like that? Who on earth has been telling you all this? It sounds like something out of a comic book!"

He drew her toward him and kissed her on the forehead. She smelled fresh and clean and it was obvious that she wanted him, so she would be more than adequate to satisfy the desires he felt.

"The last time I asked you over to stay with me, you refused, and I thought you were very cold, but I see now that I was wrong. You have a warm heart. You will save me, won't you? I can feel it. You are a man that I can trust."

She started to open the fly of his jeans.

"But what if it was me who set fire to those boxes? Surely the syndicate would be after me, too."

He did not believe a word she was saying and was not serious when he said that.

"No, you got rid of the evidence for them, so they will not try to kill you, but I saw the boxes before they burned and saw how they hid the drugs, so they will want to silence me before I can tell anyone else."

89

"How did they hide them?"

Ikuo undid her brassiere, and now that they were both naked, he carried her over to the bed in the corner of the room.

"I didn't really see anything, but they think I did. I was so pleased with the attention I was getting from the press that I pretended I knew everything, and now they are after me. But that doesn't matter now. You've got a really good body, you know. You're clever and warmhearted, too. I think I will have your child. Don't worry, I will not ask you to marry me or anything. I just want your seed. It's very 'in' to be an unmarried mother these days."

Her lips sought his, but at that moment he remembered the bruise on her thigh that she said she had received when the woman with the lion bit her.

"Is that why you slept with that woman, because it is the 'in' thing to be a lesbian?"

She did not answer him, but from the way she reacted when he entered her, he guessed that she preferred heterosexual sex.

After they had finished, he took a shower, but when he returned to the living room, he found the poodle chewing his jogging shoes. One of them was already in shreds.

"I'm really sorry. I think he must be jealous of you. He bit the laundry boy in the leg the other day, too, and gave him quite a nasty wound, although he is very quiet as a rule. I tell you what. There is a pair of sandals over there. Wear them home, and I will buy you another pair of jogging shoes later."

"Don't worry about it," he replied. "I didn't like those

90

shoes anyway. It was just that they were well broken in and comfortable to wear."

Now that he had finished doing his midnight patrols, he no longer needed jogging shoes. In fact, they were a reminder of a period he would prefer to forget, so he was not sad to see the last of them.

Even though he had just had sex with the girl in his arms, he knew that he would not like to spend the rest of his life with her. That was a feeling only Chieko instilled in him.

"I won't see you off. I want to make sure that your seed takes hold properly, so I will stay in bed a little longer. I spoke to a doctor about it, you know, and he told me this is the best way to ensure that I become pregnant. There is a key on top of the television. Let yourself out with that and keep it to come here whenever you like. If you decide that you don't want to see me again, just put it in an envelope and send it to me with some rose petals for your unborn child. Good-bye, my fireman."

"My fireman" had been Chieko's pet name for him, and it sounded strange coming from the lips of this other woman.

She kept up her melodramtic way of speech to the end, although her heart did not really seem to be in it.

6 *The Arsonist*

Michitaro hurried home from the insurance company and, going up to his room, played back a video he had recorded from a housewives' program in the afternoon. By some co-

91

incidence, his mother appeared on the program after the news, talking about the lack of exercise that children received these days, and she said that the educational system as a whole was at fault. He skimmed through that part of the program on fast forward, but he couldn't help noticing that his mother looked at least twenty years younger that day, and it was not only the effect of the television make-up she was wearing.

Finally he got to the part of the program he wanted to see. It was a reenactment of a crime the day before in which a man dressed in black clothes and red jogging shoes visited a young actress who lived alone with a pet poodle, and, after raping her, strangled her.

The actress in the reenactment put him off a bit with the enthusiasm she displayed during the rape scene, giving the whole episode a rather pornographic touch, but Michitaro was very impressed when the lion-trimmed poodle bit the intruder in the leg. It looked like a miniature lion attacking a gigantic Gulliver. He picked up his own plump poodle and hugged it to him.

"If anyone ever attacks me, I don't want you to do anything foolish like that. It will only get you killed. You should just hide in a corner until they go away and become a witness afterward. Then you will become the most famous dog in the world."

On the television, the intruder stabbed the dog with a carving knife, although the girl had been strangled, and there was not a mark on her naked body. After the murder, the intruder sprinkled gasoline around the room and, leaving a time-delay fuse, let himself out of the apartment and locked the door behind him.

After the reenactment of the crime, a reporter appeared
on the screen and started to talk in an excited voice.

"The murderer even poured gasoline on the body of the
dog that he had killed before pouring it throughout the room.
Doesn't this remind you of anything? It follows the exact
same pattern as the fire in which the lion died the other
day, and while there was no lion in this case, there was the
victim's dog that had been trimmed in a lion style at a local
pet shop the day before it died. Of course, there was nothing
found in the stomach of the dog, but the brave little animal
was found to be holding a fragment of a jogging shoe in
its teeth."

Michitaro stroked the head of the poodle in his lap, but
he was not convinced by the story.

"The most significant point is that the girl who was killed
was also an important witness in the case of the fire that
killed the lion. About a week ago she told a friend that
someone was after her, and she was so frightened that she
gave up her job in a bar and changed apartments. . . ."

The program was interrupted for a commercial advertising a low-sugar, low-salt food product and then continued
with a discussion between a criminologist and a retired
detective who had specialized in arson cases.

"The murderer left a timing device to ignite the fire after
he left, but what kind of device do you think it could have
been?" asked the criminologist, a roughly dressed man with
an open-necked shirt. "A sophisticated device such as ter-
rorists use?"

The ex-detective wore a smart suit and necktie, and chose
his words with care.

"The case is presently under investigation, so we do not

know any details, but I don't think it was anything as fancy as that. Even rental apartments are fitted with smoke detectors these days, so the fire was soon discovered and extinguished. I think there will probably be a lot of evidence left. It is unlikely that the device used was a timer."

"In that case, what kind of device do you think he used?"

"Well, when I was on the force, there was a case in which a man set fire to his house for the insurance. In order to provide himself with an alibi, he used a candle. He poured kerosene around the house before he went out and left a candle burning so that it would start the fire an hour later. That was a comparatively simple timer. But it was suspicious that the house had been left empty at the time, and as the man had stopped by his home one hour before the fire started, we were able to catch him. This is a case of murder, though, and we have to ask ourselves if it was premeditated or not. If it was not, I think it is extremely unlikely that he would happen to be carrying a timer with him."

Michitaro was impressed. He had not thought of a candle, but it was definitely the simplest form of timer. He had thought of something a bit more complicated, something much more artistic and beautiful.

"The murderer could always have gone out after he killed her to get the gasoline and a timer," the criminologist said, and the ex-detective agreed with him.

"That is true. If he poured a large amount of gasoline around the room, it is very likely that he went out to buy it. But if he did not use very much, he could always have used some benzene or stain remover that he found in the girl's apartment."

94

After the two experts had finished, it was the turn of a mystery writer to give her views.

"I think it is obvious that this is the work of an international drug ring. The last fire with the lion and this one with the poodle, . . . they were stabbed to serve as a warning, yes, a warning . . ."

But the lion had not been stabbed, Michitaro thought as he stopped the video. The only opinions worth listening to had been those put forward by the retired detective.

He let his poodle gnaw on his jogging shoes for about five minutes then phoned the television studio, saying that he had seen the afternoon program and had some questions about it.

"You said in your program that the dog was found with a fragment of a jogging shoe in its jaws, but today's jogging shoes are made of nylon and are extremely strong. I think it is unlikely that a small dog would be able to damage them very easily."

"You are quite right, sir. I must apologize, but that was something our scenario writer put in to make the story more interesting. Am I speaking to a sports-shoe manufacturer?"

He had been lucky enough to get through to the program's director, who still happened to be in the studio when he rang. He sounded very apologetic on the phone.

"You showed the murderer as wearing black clothes and red jogging shoes. Did you get that description from the police?"

"No, we dressed him in black clothes to show that we do not know what he was actually wearing. There are no witnesses, so we do not have a description of his clothes.

95

We chose red jogging shoes to stress the point that he had been wearing jogging shoes. The police said they found a man's jogging shoe on the scene, and we thought it was quite logical to assume that the other may have been taken by the dog. This was covered in the police announcement. Is there anything else?"

Michitaro was relieved to hear that the black costume had merely been a device to stress that the assailant's true appearance was unknown. When he went out to set his own fires, he always wore a black track suit, and he was scared that someone had seen him.

"Was the dog really trimmed to resemble a lion like that? There was nothing about that in the press."

"Yes, that was something our staff found out from a friend of the victim. We also checked with the shop that did the trimming, so there is no mistake."

"I'm sorry to bother you, but could you tell me the name of the shop?"

"Just a minute. I will look it up."

The producer put the phone down, but after about thirty seconds, Michitaro suddenly became worried. What if they were tracing his call? He hurriedly hung up and hugged his poodle.

It would be difficult to train this dog to act as an arsonist like the last one. It took a special kind of genius on the part of the dog to become sensitive to the smell of gasoline and carry a lighted wick over to it. His mother had already guessed what he had been trying to do, and he would look like a fool if he was to have another accident like the last one.

PART FOUR

1   *The Detective*

As Ryosaku began to climb up the steep hill, he was surrounded by the gaily dressed girls who worked in the chocolate factory. Unlike his first visit, however, he was not interested in his surroundings. He did not even glance at the sign at the bottom of the hill explaining its history, and he knew that even when he reached the top there would be no new vistas waiting for him.

Before he went into the temple, he walked around to look at the site of the condominium that was under construction nearby. The protests against the building's construction seemed to be having some effect because work had been suspended. The only person in sight was an old stonemason who was rebuilding the stone wall that stood between the temple and the building site.

Watching the old craftsman working away at his own pace, Ryosaku thought back to the conference at the station that morning. He remembered the looks some of his colleagues had given him and almost wished that he could work on his own like the old stonemason.

The consensus at the conference was that the murder of the starlet was connected with the arson cases. It was obvious that his colleagues were influenced by the press, which had drawn similarities between the poodle and the lion.

Their first inquiries revealed that a man resembling the fireman had been seen visiting her apartment shortly before the fire, and everyone wanted to know what had happened to the surveillance that was supposed to have been kept on him.

"He finally made his move. I always said that we would catch him at it again, and we had to go and lose him," said the detective who was two years his senior and usually friendly toward Ryosaku.

Ryosaku, knowing he was at fault, just sat in silence with his head bowed. When he had seen the fireman buy some noodles as usual, he thought that he had just enough time, while the other was eating his noodles, to go to a store and buy some perfume for Chieko. He wanted to complain that his partner had been late and that he should already have been off duty, but he knew that it would not wash because it was his duty to wait until he had actually been relieved.

"As far as we were able to tell, there was no evidence that the fireman ever left his room that night after he returned from duty," he said weakly. In fact, for some reason his partner did not see Ikuo return to his room either, so he was not exactly lying, but he knew that due to their laziness, they were in fact providing an alibi for the man. They had both expected him to eat his noodles and then sleep for the rest of the night as he usually did, and they had allowed themselves to be put off their guard.

In an effort to cheer himself up, he had come to the temple to investigate the statue he had found. This was a trump card that only he held.

The chief priest did not seem to be very pleased to see him, especially after he heard that he was not there to copy the sutras this time.

"Can you tell me the names of the stonemasons whom you employ in the temple, please?"

"If you want to see the mason, he is working up at the back of the temple at the moment. He does all our work for us on his own."

Seeing the chief priest's suspicious look, he guessed that the young priest was at the root of it, but thanking him politely, he left and made his way back up the hill to where he had seen the mason at work.

"Excuse me, I wonder if you could answer one or two questions," he said, showing the stonemason his identification. "I have checked it with the chief priest."

The man seemed to be ready enough to talk.

"What can I do for you?"

"It is about the statue of a lion over there. Did you carve it?"

"Yes, that was me."

"Who commissioned you to do it?"

"The temple. They gave me a photograph to copy, but I was not particularly pleased with the result."

"What, a picture of a lion?"

"A lion? No, that was a poodle, not a lion. It was a very expensive dog, but it died in a fire. The owner doted on it like a child, and they said they wanted the statue for a

99

memorial. It was cropped to look like a lion, but a dog is a dog. It was a real job to carve! The owner said that it was to be made identical to the photograph. It took ages to do, and it did not pay very well."

He did not seem to mind the detective's questions at all. He appeared to be completely indifferent to the outside world and could not care less about arsonists or murderers.

"Didn't you meet the person who owned the dog at all?"

"No, they dealt directly with the temple. I only spoke to them on the phone. It was a woman. She sounded like a real nag."

"How old would you say she was?"

"I don't know. As I said, I only talked to her on the phone. Perhaps you had better ask at the temple."

A note of caution crept into his voice.

"Do you have any idea when the statue was removed?"

"You'll have to ask that at the temple, too. I think it was the young priest who was in charge of it. The memorial period was probably finished, so they took it away."

He turned back to his job, and Ryosaku was about to leave when he thought of one more question.

"About the photograph of the dog you used. Could I borrow it for a while?"

The mason paused for a moment then replied without looking up.

"I will have to look for it when I get home."

As he made his way back to the temple, Ryosaku could not help but feel disappointed. He had been convinced that the statue had been of a lion, but he had been off the mark.

He told the chief priest that he would like to talk to his assistant again, but he learned that he had gone to the

Ministry of the Environment with some of the local people
to protest against the construction of the condominium.

"In that case, could you please lend me the records of
everyone who has copied sutras here recently? I would like
to copy some of them."

He did not say anything about the statue of the poodle.

"If you need it for your work, you are welcome to use
the copier in the temple."

The priest seemed to have warmed toward him again.

"This is the one I want to copy, the one by Ikuo Onda.
It's the same name as the fireman whose I.D. was found in
the stomach of the lion that died in a fire," he explained.

"I see, so that is why you made all that fuss about the
statue of a lion that you said you saw on the temple grounds,
is it? What did the mason tell you? Was he able to be of
any help?"

"It was not a statue of a lion after all. It was a poodle
that had been trimmed to resemble one."

"I wonder who put it there?" the old priest said,
frowning.

"I don't know, but I would appreciate it if you could
find out." He produced a picture of Ikuo Onda. "Is this the
man who copied the sutra?"

"I am afraid I cannot help you there. I was in Kyoto that
day. I spend half my time in Kyoto, you know."

Just the same, he put on his glasses and looked at the
picture.

Ryosaku left the temple feeling very disappointed. He
had not been able to learn anything new, and he wondered
if he was barking up the wrong tree. The statue of a lion,
which had first made him feel that the temple was connected

with the case, had turned out to be a poodle, and it would appear that he had just been wasting his time.

He walked up the hill toward Meguro station, and, as he did, he passed a woman wearing sunglasses whom he felt he knew from somewhere. For a moment he felt that it was someone from his childhood, but then he realized it was a famous educationalist who often appeared on television.

He turned to take another look at her and was just in time to see her walk through the temple gate. He wondered idly if she had come to the temple on purpose or whether she had been in the area and had just stopped by to look at the famous statues, but he was not really interested either way. He walked a bit farther and came to a sign outside a hotel announcing a seminar on modern education in Japan, and he felt thankful that he did not have any children. Only that morning, one of his colleagues had been complaining that it was very difficult to get his son into a good university.

2   *The Fireman*

Ikuo came off duty, and, after basking in the sun in a nearby park, he went into the bar of the local hotel. It was still only ten o'clock in the morning, but, as usual, a number of foreigners were there drinking. He could not understand why they would want to be drinking at that time of day until he realized that like him they had probably been up all night and had just arrived in Tokyo. He guessed that they probably needed the alcohol to help them unwind before they went to bed.

Then his thoughts turned to Chieko and her sleeping

pills. He wondered if she still used them and guessed that she did. Now that there was no man beside her when she slept, he doubted whether her pill consumption had risen very much. What had risen, though, was the amount of alcohol he drank.

He wanted to drink some saké, but he settled for a bourbon and soda. This way he would be better able to keep his guard up when he met the reporter.

"I'm ten minutes late. I'm very sorry. It doesn't do to keep a V.I.P. like you waiting," the reporter said impenetrably when he finally arrived. "Actually, I met a detective I know over there. He is following you, so he looked a bit put out when he saw me. I told him that I had come to interview you and that I had an appointment for one hour. He looked very relieved and disappeared. I guess he thought there would be no need to watch you if you were with me. They don't want you to know they are following you. They hope that if they follow you long enough, you are going to set another fire and then they will have you."

The man had once been a crime reporter, and he seemed to know what he was talking about.

"But I killed some time in the park before I came here, and yet I did not see anyone," said Ikuo.

"They have probably increased the number of men they have got watching you; either that or they are using a car. Although the official stance is that there is no connection between the death of that starlet and the fire with the lion, they don't really believe that, and they are going all out to catch the man who did it. They don't have much choice the way the press are capitalizing on it."

He went on to say that everyone suspected Ikuo of being

responsible, as his I.D. had been found in the lion's stomach, but he didn't agree with the others. He ordered a tomato juice and silently toasted Ikuo with it.

"However, on the day that the starlet was murdered, you were off duty and in your room asleep. The police were watching you, so you have a perfect alibi. It is only because the press are making all these allegations that they are still watching you at all. You should sue for defamation of character. I will introduce you to a good lawyer if you like."

The reporter kept on chatting away excitedly, but Ikuo just sat silently and watched the bubbles in his drink as they rose to the top of the glass.

Did the police watch on him really provide him with an alibi? Now that he came to think about it, he realized this must be the case because they still had not come to question him about his actions that night. After he had left the starlet's room wearing her sandals, he had taken a cab home and gone straight to bed. He had never even dreamed that she would be murdered and her apartment set on fire.

All he did know was that someone had tried to set him up. Why had his I.D. and driver's license been found in the stomach of the lion? Why had he been lured over to the starlet's room with sex as the bait and his jogging shoes used to incriminate him once again? If the police were to ask him about his jogging shoes, what could he answer? If he were to tell them the truth, he would be made a laughing-stock. He decided to keep silent about the whole matter.

Before he had met the reporter, he had wanted to tell someone the truth, but now he realized that it would be best if he were just to remain quiet. The reporter's story about the police providing him with an alibi sounded quite plausible. Not only did the reporter know what he was talking about, but the fact that the police had not asked him about his jogging shoes was proof.

"Anyway, I am on your side, don't forget that. If you think of leaving the fire brigade or taking a long period off, let me know first, O.K.? For my part, I will keep an eye on the police, and, if worst comes to worst, I can always introduce you to a lawyer."

Seeing that Ikuo was not going to say anything useful, the reporter stood up.

"Oh yes, the police are checking up on your background, you know. Have you got any girlfriends or a fiancée? It's no good trying to hide anything, you know."

"No, I have not," the fireman replied firmly, looking the reporter straight in the eye.

"O.K., I'll be off then. But remember, if anything happens, if you are about to be arrested, just get in touch with me and leave everything in our hands. It is the only hope you have got."

The reporter took the bill and headed for the door. Then he stopped and returned.

"If, just supposing, you are the arsonist, please get in touch if you are arrested. I can guarantee that we will pay more than anyone else for your story."

Ikuo ordered another whiskey and knocked it down in one gulp, but it did not make him feel any better, and he realized that he would not be able to sleep a wink that day. He knew that the best thing for him would be to go to the police and tell them the whole story, but there was the danger that they would not believe him and arrest him on the spot.

No, he would have to try to catch the arsonist himself while he was still free to do so. The next day with a five in it was only three days away, and the arsonist had not made a move for a month now. The day the starlet had been killed had not had a five in it, and for some reason that gave him a strange sense of satisfaction.

He left the bar and went out into the lobby of the hotel to buy a newspaper. He noticed a young couple walking toward him. The girl was the daughter of the Fire Chief whom he had once been introduced to, but he did not recognize the pale man in the well-made suit. Their eyes met and he bowed slightly toward the girl, but she only made the slightest nod in reply and seemed to want to avoid him.

He looked through the newspapers and had just decided which ones he wanted to buy when the girl came back to him.

"How have you been?" she said. "I'm sorry to bother you, but if you have the time my friend is very eager to talk to you. I hope you don't mind me asking you like this."

She smiled at him guilelessly, and he felt that he would like to talk to someone else before he went home. Thinking of the police who were somewhere invisibly watching him, he felt that he would like to talk to a person of flesh and blood. No matter how senseless a conversation it might turn out to be, he needed to talk to someone.

"Not at all. As it happens, I have some time to kill, so I would be delighted to talk to your friend."

So saying, he put the newspapers he had just chosen back on the rack where he had found them.

3   *The Arsonist*

Michitaro stood in a corner of the lobby, watching the girl talking to the fireman who was suspected of being the arsonist. For some reason he had suddenly felt overwhelmed by an urge to talk to this fireman who now was not only suspected of being the arsonist, but also of being a murderer. He watched them, doubting that the fireman would agree to talk, but then to his surprise he saw the girl lead him over. His pulse started to race.

"I'm sorry to drag you over like this, but when I heard that this young lady was an acquaintance of yours, I just had to meet you," he said in a friendly voice as he led him into the coffee bar in a corner of the lobby. He thought the fireman looked a bit gaunt, but Ikuo was friendly and returned the greeting affably.

"This is an admirable young lady, you know. There are all kinds of rumors flying around about you, but she refuses to take sides and treats us both as equal suitors for her hand."

Despite the girl's obvious embarrassment, he spoke about his prospects for marrying her and watched the fireman's reaction closely. But Ikuo failed to register any emotion, and Michitaro started to feel antagonistic toward him. *Perhaps this man really did kill the actress*, he thought.

"Actually, I work for the company that insured the circus lion that ate your I.D. card, and I wanted to talk to you about the policy that had been taken out on the animal."

He watched Ikuo's reactions carefully as he lifted his

teacup. He was an expert at gauging people's reactions. It was a game he had played with his mother every day ever since he could remember, and this time the fireman looked genuinely surprised.

"I didn't know the lion had been insured. You would have thought that with the fuss the papers are making about the case, one of them would have mentioned it." Ikuo looked over at Michitaro with a renewed interest, thinking that perhaps he had found a new ally in this young insurance executive.

"Well, actually the policy was made out with the owner as the sole beneficiary, and there was a clause that stated that if she were to die, the policy would become void. There was a huge sum involved, but as the woman died, the company didn't suffer at all. The thing is, however, I have to investigate it and decide whether it was an accident caused by a random case of arson or whether it was done in an effort to defraud the company, and that's why I wanted to talk to you."

"If it wasn't an accident, what do you suggest?" Ikuo asked seriously.

"We must always consider the possibility that the woman lit the fire herself and then let the lion out of its cage. Normally, lions are very docile animals. Except when it's the mating season, they very rarely attack humans. When wild animals escape from a zoo, everyone is very scared of them, but in reality, they just want to find somewhere to hide, away from human beings. This is all recorded in a famous book called *Animals Kept in Civilization* by a well-known zoologist. Nevertheless, in the case of a fire or some other tragedy, the animals panic and attack anything in sight, so it is only natural for the police to shoot such an animal. There is always the chance that the woman thought of this and then let the animal out of its cage, knowing that it would be shot but that no suspicion would fall on her."

He made a point of showing how wide his knowledge of the subject was in order to impress the girl and the fireman.

"You mean that she started the fire herself?"

"Yes, she could have started the fire herself in order to collect the insurance on the lion. But either she was too drunk or she waited too long before she started to make her escape and perished in the fire, making the insurance policy void. At least that would give some kind of meaning to the death of the woman and the lion, don't you agree?"

He looked the fireman in the eye, waiting for confirmation of his theory. If the fire could be put down to attempted fraud, he did not have to fear the police ever investigating him, and the poor fireman who was being made into a scapegoat for him would also be let off the hook.

"Do you think the police would agree with your theory?" asked the fireman.

"Why not? After all, when you tried to persuade her to clear away the boxes, she was very antagonistic toward you and drove you away. Couldn't that have been because she needed those boxes to start the fire?"

"I suppose so, but that fire was only one in a whole series of arson attacks. Do you mean to say that she was responsible for all of them?"

"It is quite feasible. The other fires could have been started to act as camouflage. If her house was the only one to be burned down, we would suspect her of fraud right away, but if it was only one in a whole chain of similar events, everyone would think it was the work of an arsonist. Well, that is one way of looking at it, but there are still some things that remain to be explained. For instance, why were your I.D. and driver's license found inside the lion's stomach? Do you have any idea?"

"If I knew the answer to that, I wouldn't be in the trouble I am now."

"From my knowledge of animals, I would say that it is very unlikely that the lion would have eaten it of its own accord. The only way I could think of getting the lion to eat it would be for the owner to wrap it in meat or something that the lion particularly liked and then feed it to him. I suppose she found your wallet after you had left and fed it to the lion to spite you. I don't think we should attach too much importance to it anyway."

Ikuo sat staring into space while he thought over what the other had said. Michitaro felt like teasing him some more and almost told him about his poodle that had been trimmed to resemble a lion and that had died in a fire, too, but he realized he would be pushing his luck too far. Instead, he decided to tell him about an event from his childhood.

"My interest in fires is not merely professional, you know. When I was a child in nursery school, I think I must have been about five, some friends and I were playing with matches, and the house caught fire. My father was asleep in bed upstairs after having taken some sleeping pills, and he died in the blaze. It was a terrible shock to have to suffer at such a young age, and even now I can remember the ache whenever I hear that someone has died in a fire."

He watched the girl and the fireman closely to gauge

their reactions, and he was not disappointed. They both looked stunned, and, in particular, the fireman stared at him in amazement and seemed about to say something, but then he changed his mind and dropped his eyes.

"I never knew that your father died like that," the girl said. "I had heard that he died of an illness."

"Yes, we don't like to talk about it very much. There was some doubt about the cause of death, as he would appear to have died before the flames reached him, but it was put down to carbon monoxide poisoning or shock—he was not very strong, you know. Either way, there was no doubt that he died in the fire, and my mother received a large amount of money from the insurance company.

"My father refused to join the family business, you know, and went off to France to study painting, so he was disowned by my grandfather. He also married my mother and had me against the protests of the family, so we have very little to do with the rest of the family now."

Michitaro was surprised that he should be talking about these things. He could understand why he would want to tell the girl, who might very well become his wife one day, but not the fireman, whom he had never even met before that day.

4   *The Detective*

Ryosaku found himself in the elevator with a crowd of young office girls as he went to visit the offices of the insurance company. He found that being in such close contact with so many beautiful young women aroused him ever so slightly, but none of them could compare with Chieko.

He stopped for a minute at the door of the executive offices, feeling a bit overpowered by the obvious wealth of the company. He had to remind himself that he was an important public servant, representing the general populace, or he would have felt at a disadvantage when he met the grandson of the owner.

The Chief Inspector had personally given him this chance to redeem himself after the mess he had made of following the fireman, and although he could not understand why such an important person would take the trouble to help him like that, he felt that the least he could do was to make a good job of it and justify the other's faith in him.

"I am here about the insurance policy on the lion. How much was it insured for?"

He came straight to the point of his visit.

"It was not very much, but where did you hear about it?"

The man who answered him was about his own age, and he sat nonchalantly at a highly polished mahogany desk.

"We get all kinds of tips from the general public, and although a great deal of it comes to nothing, we have to follow it all up."

"I am afraid that the man who dealt with the policy is out of the office at the moment, but if I can be of any assistance . . ." He looked down at some papers he was holding in his hand. "According to this, the lion was insured for the period it was to appear on the television, and the policy was designed to cover the cost of finding another lion should there be an accident during the filming. It was taken out by the TV company, and the company is the sole beneficiary."

Michitaro looked over the neatly typed policy once more before offering it to the detective.

"Since the lion died before the filming started, this policy became void."

Looking over the copy, Ryosaku saw that he was right.

"You can have a copy of the policy if you like, although I don't suppose it will be very much use to you." Seeing the look of disappointment on the detective's face, he added, "It is very strange about the fireman's I.D. being found in the lion's stomach like that, though, isn't it? How do you suppose it got there? They are writing all kinds of things in the magazines, but what do the police think?"

Ryosaku realized that he owed it to the insurance man to go through the standard story about the state of their inquiries again.

"We don't attach much importance to what is written in the magazines, and pursue each case from a variety of angles. It makes no difference to us whose documents may have been found in the stomach of the lion."

"I agree. If it was that fireman who started the fire, I think it very unlikely that he would purposely leave his I.D. in the lion's stomach to advertise what he had done. I feel quite sorry for the poor man."

Ryosaku merely nodded politely but did not say anything, so Michitaro continued.

"From experience, I would say that it would be very difficult for anyone other than the owner to force an animal to eat someone's I.D. like that. They would have to coat it in honey or something else that the animal particularly liked, but even so I think it would be extremely difficult."

113

"Oh, do you keep a lion then?" Ryosaku asked, unable to restrain himself.

"Oh no, but I do have a poodle that has been trimmed like one." He laughed. "Wouldn't you say that a poodle looks just like a miniature lion? Not that I have ever seen the real thing, you understand."

Ryosaku thought back to the photograph he had seen of the poodle that had died in the starlet's apartment. The body and legs had been cropped leaving a long mane, and it looked very artificial. Personally, he liked long-haired dogs and had been disgusted by what he had seen.

"No, I wouldn't. For one thing the color is completely different. It has just had its hair cropped like that to amuse us humans. But it was a coincidence that the actress who was murdered had a poodle like that. Do you think there is any connection?"

He looked at Michitaro questioningly.

"I don't know, but surely that was a murder case, not arson. Yet I remember reading that the girl was to appear in a play on television with the lion so maybe there is some connection between them."

"I see," Ryosaku said, and stood up to go. Even if he thought that the two cases might be connected, he had no way of proving it.

Michitaro also stood up and followed him out to the corridor.

"My girlfriend is the daughter of the Fire Chief, you know. It must be very difficult for him at the moment with this arsonist on the loose."

"No, it's the police who are having a hard time."

"She dated that fireman a couple of times, too, you know.

Apparently he is a very good fireman, and it seems a shame that he should be accused of arson like that."

Ryosaku agreed and wondered if most people sympathized with the fireman like that. Personally he was convinced that the fireman was guilty of both of the arson cases and of the starlet's murder and felt very antagonistic toward him.

"Anyway, I hope you catch this man soon. They say the Japanese police are among the best in the world," Michitaro said seriously as he held out his hand.

Ryosaku felt obliged to shake hands in the western style and guessed wrongly that the insurance man had probably spent quite a length of time abroad.

As he went down in the elevator, he felt that he knew the insurance man from somewhere, and the feel of his hand seemed to awaken memories from his childhood. His thoughts soon came back to the present, however, and he realized that the insurance man was the son of the educationalist he had seen outside the temple in Meguro.

He had found the educationalist's book of correspondence with her son among his dead wife's belongings, and there had been a photograph of the mother and son on the cover. He had read it through, but the main impression he received was that his wife, who had died during pregnancy, had probably wanted a son. He guessed that the child who had been described in the book would have never wanted for anything, and now that they had met, he realized there was something artificial about him, like a clipped poodle.

Suddenly the insurance man's reference to a clipped poodle came back to him. He remembered seeing the man's mother walking into the temple at Meguro and thought of the stonemason who had told him that the statue had been ordered by a woman. All these things came together in his mind for the moment, but that was as far as it went. It seemed to be too much of a coincidence to mean anything, and he pushed the idea away into a corner of his brain.

5   The Fireman

The sound of the telephone ringing brought Ikuo out of a deep sleep, and for a moment he thought that it was the police coming to arrest him, but it was only Chieko calling. In his dream he was being interrogated by the police, but the person in charge of the investigation resembled his mother, and he was only five years old.

.   "Are you phoning from the hospital? I will ring you back, this phone might be bugged," he said. He was still half asleep, but he noticed a strange noise on the line.

"Don't be silly. The Japanese police don't bug people's phones like that. How are you feeling? You sound exhausted."

"Oh, I'm fine."

"That's good. It said in the news that it was only a matter of time before you are arrested, and I was very worried about you. I thought we might not be able to see each other again."

"Don't worry about what they say in the news. They don't know what they're talking about."

"But what about your I.D. card? They say it was found in the stomach of the lion. Have you heard anything about that?"

"I reported its loss to my superior at the fire station, and apparently he had heard something from the police."

"The police have been around to see me, you know. They asked me all kinds of questions, but I didn't tell them anything. I said that you had stayed with me that night."

"I won't cause you any trouble. I've made up my mind that I won't go to your place again. I sent your key back in the mail."

"I know. I got it. But don't hesitate to come around anytime you feel like it. No matter what anyone else says, I believe in you."

Ikuo remained silent. He realized that he would never visit her room again, and a gulf seemed to open between them. There could be no going back.

"There is one thing I must know," he said. "Did I really take my wallet with me when I left you that night? I cannot help but feel that I left it on your dresser."

He knew it was a meaningless question, but it had been worrying him ever since he first discovered that it was missing, and it took a weight off his mind to get it out into the open.

Chieko replied with a slightly hysterical laugh.

"Are you sure you are all right? Of course you took it with you. I think that all those things they have written about you in the papers have made you a bit neurotic. You should come into the hospital and have a checkup. There is a very good doctor here, and I'm sure he could help you. You haven't been suffering from any severe headaches or vomiting, have you? If you come to the hospital, we can give you a scan and soon be able to find out if you have a tumor or something."

She sounded quite serious, and he thanked her for her

advice, but then, realizing that she wanted to go on speaking, he quietly put the phone down. Although the voice was the same, she seemed to be a completely different person from the one who had wished him luck when he went out on his night patrols.

He went to the fridge and, taking out a can of beer, he downed it all in one go. He wondered whether there was in fact a tumor growing in his skull, but then he went back to bed without giving the matter any further thought.

The next morning, he considered going to the hospital as the nurse had suggested, but then he thought better of it and went to the library instead. He went into the room where they kept copies of all the old newspapers and took out the binders that contained the papers from March to June of the year when he had been five years old.

He found that he was unable to forget what the insurance man had said about his having been involved in a fire as a child. He could still remember Michitaro's face from all those years ago, but he could not believe that the insurance man was the same person. He had almost blurted out that he had been one of the other children who had been playing with him, but he stopped himself and decided to check it out at the library first.

Although his memory of that time was rather fragmentary, it still came back to him clearly. They had gone to Michitaro's house to look at his tadpoles. There had been several of them in a large aquarium, and, although Ikuo had wanted one, too, Michitaro was the only one who ever had any pocket money to buy things. It was because of the tadpoles that he guessed the fire had occurred in the spring.

He leafed through the papers and soon came to a large

photograph of the fire in the March 22 edition. To begin with, the papers merely said that the fire had started in the home of the son of the founder of an insurance company and that the cause was unknown, but as time passed it became obvious that it had been caused by the man's young son and his friends who had been playing with matches. The children had all claimed they had seen a man dressed like a bat running up the stairs breathing flames, but their story was considered to be a lie they had concocted to prove their innocence. Looking back at that period now, he realized they had told all sorts of lies in those days, but strangely enough, he felt that he really had seen the man they described running up the stairs.

He picked up a box of matches that someone had left lying on the table and struck one. He sat there without moving until his fingers started to get hot. Something stirred in his memory.

They had struck lots of matches and left them in piles around the house, on the carpet in the living room, in the hall, on the stairs, but they had put all of them out with water from the aquarium holding the tadpoles. The idea of the game had been to collect the dead matches, but who was it who had gone up to the second floor to make a pile of matchsticks there? Had it been him? Had they known that Michitaro's father was up there? But yes, he had seen him, a man lying almost completely nude with his legs open . . .

His fingers suddenly started to burn, and he hurriedly dropped the match to the floor. He looked down and saw to his surprise that there were already several matches lying there, burned all the way to the end.

He went over to the water cooler and had a drink. The past had come back to him all too vividly, and he walked back toward the reference room almost like a man in a trance. When he entered the room, he saw a man of about his own age standing in front of the papers he had left open on the desk, gazing at them like a man possessed.

As he drew nearer, the man moved away, but as he did so he threw Ikuo a wistful glance.

6   *The Arsonist*

Michitaro had taken a cold shower to drive all the unnecessary thoughts from his mind, but it was not working. He still could not rid himself of the unease he felt over the police visit to his office.

It had been lucky that the girl in the public relations department had happened to be busy when they phoned and the call had been put through to him, or he would never have known about it. He had been able to palm the detective off with the small policy that the TV company had taken out on the lion, but he could not be sure that the detective had believed him. Certainly the detective could not know about the other policy. It was top secret and its existence was only known to a mere handful of executives in the company. Nobody would want to have anything to do with that policy now, and his grandmother, who was the real boss of the company, would not even want to hear about it. He thought he had done the right thing, if only he could be sure that the detective would not suspect anything. He did not want to have anything to do with the police at all and felt much safer if he could keep out of their way altogether. He wished now that he had not mentioned his poodle. He should have just answered the detective's questions and got rid of him as soon as possible.

Next his thoughts went to his girlfriend. At least he seemed to be doing all right in that regard. In fact, if anything he was doing too well. The other day, he had pulled into the parking lot of a motel on their way back from Yokohama. He had only meant it as a joke, but she had taken him seriously.

"I have nothing against premarital sex. If the people involved love each other, they should be willing to show it at any place or time. They may never have the chance again."

Hearing her talk like this, he had no option but to play the experienced playboy and lead her up to a room. They embraced naked in bed, and in a few more moments it would have become obvious that he had never done this before, but he said, "I am quite old-fashioned in some ways, you know, and I think that if we are going to be married, we should restrain ourselves until the vows have been read and we are ready to have children."

He let her see that she aroused him physically, then he moved away. He did not think she realized he was still a virgin. At least she would not have been able to tell that, whenever he was alone with a girl, he felt as if his mother's hands were digging into his shoulders and holding him back. She had seen that he was a virile man, and he felt sure that once they got married and went on their honeymoon he would be able to have sex without any problems.

* * *

He opened the foreign pornographic magazine he had brought into the bathroom with him and looked hungrily at the pictures of blond girls sitting with their legs spread while he played with himself.

Once he had satisfied himself that there was nothing physically wrong with him, he had another cold shower and opened the bathroom door.

The moment the door swung open, he saw two strange men in navy blue combat fatigues and ski masks. They both had pistols trained on him.

"Don't make a sound. If you say anything, we'll shoot."

The man spoke in a calm voice while his companion handcuffed Michitaro. They covered his naked body with a black cape and led him to his bedroom where they collected his wallet, driver's license, watch, and other items that he customarily carried with him.

Michitaro was convinced that the two men were policemen, and his teeth chattered with fear. Somehow they had found out that he was the arsonist and had come to arrest him. He had had nightmares about this moment for years, and now it had come.

At that moment, his poodle came into the room. Sensing his master's predicament, he bit one of the two men in the leg. The man turned his gun on the hapless dog. There was a small popping sound, and the animal lay dead at his feet. The men's guns were fitted with silencers!

At that moment, Michitaro realized that these were not the defenders of society come to arrest him, but kidnappers.

"If you resist, you'll get the same as the dog," said the man who had not fired.

The man spoke in such a calm voice that Michitaro wondered if they worked for some agency other than the police, a kind of Japanese FBI or something.

"What do you want?" he asked in a hoarse voice.

"We are kidnapping you for ransom. If you behave sensibly and do what you are told, you will soon be a free man. Now don't speak again."

To show that he was serious, he hit Michitaro on the shoulder with the butt of his gun. Although the pain was enough to make Michitaro cry out, he was filled with a feeling of relief. They were dressed like riot police and spoke with the assurance of men who had been well trained, but they were not the police. His crimes had still not been found out, and he wanted to cry for joy.

They went down to the garage in the basement, and, ignoring his sports car, they went to his mother's limousine, which he also used when he went out on his fire-raising missions, and opened the trunk. In one corner of the trunk, he saw the black fatigues and jogging shoes he had put there that day and realized, with a sense of foreboding, that he had meant to go out again later on.

How did they know so much about his house? They moved around as if they owned the place, and even though his mother was appearing on TV at that time, he could not understand why they acted so confidently.

"Lie down and be quiet. One sound and we'll dump the car at the bottom of a lake."

The men slammed the lid of the trunk, and it became pitch black. He could smell gasoline, and he guessed that the drawstring on the top of the rubber bag of gasoline had come loose, but he could not do anything about it. He thought of himself being burned to death, naked in the trunk of the car, and it was not a very nice idea.

The men had said that he was to be held for ransom, but he wondered just who was supposed to pay. His father and grandfather were already dead, and his grandmother, who possessed all the money in the family, had disowned Michitaro and his mother and had promised all her money to medical and religious organizations. He only held the position in the company that he did out of respect for his grandfather, and he did not know if the company would be prepared to pay the ransom fee. Perhaps his grandmother would forget her dislike of him and his mother now that he had been kidnapped. After all, he was her flesh and blood. At the very least, he was entitled to his legal portion of her estate under the inheritance laws.

The car started to move, and maybe because he was exhausted after masturbating in the bathroom earlier he fell into a deep sleep. The only thing that really worried him was the fact that he had left the pornographic magazine in the bathroom where his mother might find it.

PART
FIVE

1   *The Detective*

When Ryosaku heard that Michitaro had been kidnapped, his first thought was that this time it was not his fault. He did not realize that he might have made a mistake until he was summoned in front of the Chief Inspector and told that Michitaro was being threatened over the insurance policy on the lion.

"You reported that the lion was only insured for the period it was to appear on the TV and that the policy had been taken out by the TV company for a minimal sum, but it would appear that it goes much deeper than you thought. That woman had insured the lion for a huge sum, with herself as the sole beneficiary, but because she died the insurance company refused to pay, and now some of her associates have kidnapped the founder's grandson and say they will not return him alive unless they are paid the full sum due to them."

The Chief Inspector gave him a look of pity.

"But when I went to the company, they didn't mention anything like—"

"Yes, I know. The company had kept the existence of the policy top secret, and we didn't find out about it until we received the ransom note, so it was not your fault. Nevertheless, you had a chance. It was you who went to investigate the policy."

"Do we have any idea who the people are?"

"No. That woman doesn't have any relatives in Japan. Her husband was a Frenchman. He was a trapeze artist in a circus, but he died in an accident. She was already a rich woman, and she didn't leave any heirs."

"Then surely it is a little strange that the kidnappers should be demanding the insurance payment, isn't it?"

"Yes, I told you that things ran deep in this case. The victim was missing for a week before we got a ransom note, but his mother and the people in his office all thought he had just gone off without telling anyone. It was his mother who first said so. She's a funny one. Perhaps you have heard of her. She has made quite a name for herself as an authority on education. Anyway, she comes home, finds her son missing, their pet poodle shot, and then insists he has left home. She thought he had killed the dog himself in order to spite her. She also found a foreign pornographic magazine in the bathroom, and, as both pornography and guns are forbidden in this country, she assumes he was showing his disregard for the law. She is trying to keep up her image as a well-known personality, but it is obvious she cannot think straight and doesn't know what she is saying."

"Was the poodle trimmed to resemble a lion?" asked Ryosaku.

The Chief Inspector gave him a quizzical look.

"No, the dog was untrimmed, but after it was killed, the mother took it to the local pet shop and had it trimmed like a lion before it was buried!"

"I see. I thought that might be the case. Am I to join the kidnap investigation?"

"No. You are to stick with the arson case. I want you to stick to it on your own, and in particular I don't want you to let that fireman out of your sight."

"Yes, sir."

He dropped his gaze to the floor. He could not understand why his superior should be so adamant about his pursuit of the fireman.

"For the time being, I want you to forget you are a policeman. I want you to think of yourself as a private detective who has been given a case and apply yourself to it one hundred percent."

Ryosaku was silent.

"You must have read some foreign detective books," continued the Chief Inspector. "I want you to be like one of the private eyes in the movies, to think about nothing but the fireman and the arson cases twenty-four hours a day. You must stick to him as if your life depended on it. You will be on your own, not part of a team, and I want you to report to me, and me alone."

"I understand, sir."

Ryosaku walked to the door and then he turned.

"Would you like me to hand in my resignation, sir?"

"Don't be stupid. Just do this my way. You won't have to take any of the responsibility. It's something I want to do. I will be up for retirement soon and before I leave, I want to do something my way for a change. You often hear about policemen acting in a thoroughly unpolicemanlike manner, robbing someone or selling their driver's license. To read about it in the press, you would think they were the devil incarnate, but they are only human. Well, for once in my life, I want to act in an unpolicemanlike way, too. I feel that if we go about this case in the normal way, we will not get anywhere with it, so I want you to do it my way. I will take full responsibility, and you don't have to worry about what your colleagues or superiors might say."

He looked at him fondly, and a smile brightened his features.

"Actually . . ." Ryosaku was about to tell him that the fireman, the insurance man, and he had all been involved in a fire as children, but then he realized that somehow the Chief Inspector already knew, which was why he was giving him this job. As a rule he would not even be able to speak to the Chief Inspector directly, and just because the other had chosen to reveal a facet of his real self was no reason for him to do the same. He came to attention and, saluting, left the room and closed the door.

He went straight to the hospital to see Chieko. He stood in the waiting room until she finished work, and he saw her walking toward him in that straight-backed, fast walk that was the badge of her profession.

"I wondered if you would like to come out to dinner with me, if you have the time, that is."

"Only if you promise me some more Italian wine."

She looked very tired, but she rewarded him with a professional smile. He did not care if she meant it or not. After all, he was now a private detective in a foreign movie.

"Of course, I wasn't expecting you to treat me to your special wine again," he said.

"That's O.K., I still have half a bottle left."

As they left the hospital, she took his arm, and he reflected that they had finished her wine the last time he visited her. He guessed that she must be feeling lonely.

They sat down in an Italian restaurant, and after drinking a glass of Chianti, he gazed at the flame of the candle on their table.

"There is something I would like to tell you about your boyfriend. It is half a police secret and half personal."

"I don't want to hear anything about that person," she said, shaking her head.

"It is nothing to do with you. It is about the past when we were five years old and were still attending nursery school."

"We? Do you know him then?"

"I did not realize it at first, but we were childhood friends. We went to nursery school together, but our primary schools were different. After the fire, his parents found it too humiliating to remain in the area and they moved away."

"What fire?" She drank her Chianti and sat watching him closely as he spoke.

"We were playing with matches and there was a large fire. A person died."

"Did he start the fire?"

"I can't remember. I was only five and my memory is blurred. In fact, I don't think I really knew what happened even then."

He ate an eggplant that had been fried in olive oil,

wondering if what he said was the truth or whether he really had known at the time.

He felt an almost overwhelming desire to bury his face in her lap and admit that it was he who had started the fire. If his mother had been living when he was five, he would probably have confessed to her, but she was already dead at the time.

"The Chief Inspector called me in today and instructed me to devote myself entirely to watching Ikuo, but I did not tell him we used to be friends."

"Does Ikuo know who you are?"

"I doubt it. In fact I don't think he even knows I am following him. People don't remember nearly so much about their childhood as they would like to think. For instance, do you remember the name of the person you sat next to first at school?"

After they finished their meal, it seemed the most natural thing in the world that they should go back to her apartment.

"Now that I know you both used to be friends, it makes me feel like a prostitute," she whispered in his ear as she got into bed naked with him. "But what happened to the third boy who had been there during the fire? What is he doing now?"

"If you had slept with him, too, you really would look like a prostitute, but there is no need to worry. Things like that only happen in fairy tales."

He almost told her that the third boy was the victim of a kidnapping, but decided against it. He lay fondling her breast absently as he thought of his childhood friend who was now in the hands of a group of kidnappers. If he was released and the restrictions on the press coverage were canceled, he would be in the headlines like Ikuo. That would mean that two of the three children had become famous.

The nurse reached down to his thighs, and feeling her warm breath on his stomach he found that he could no longer concentrate on the fate of his childhood friend.

2   *The Fireman*

"There is a phone call for you. It is from a girl," Ikuo's superior said, frowning, as he handed him the phone.

He could not imagine who it could be. He had told Chieko that she was never to phone him at work, and although for a moment he thought it might be the Fire Chief's daughter, the voice was different. It was a brisk, businesslike voice. After checking and rechecking that she was indeed talking to Ikuo Onda, she told him that she was transferring the call. There was a click, and a man came on the line.

"Hello, I don't know if you remember me, but I met you in the lobby of a hotel recently. I was with the daughter of the Fire Chief and I told you I worked for an insurance company."

"Yes, I remember. What do you want?" He could not imagine why Michitaro would want to phone him.

"I'm sorry to phone you at work, but I'm afraid it's a matter of life and death, and I would be very grateful if you could hear me out. I assume this call is not being taped."

"Of course it is not, but I would appreciate it if you could keep it brief."

"Of course. I don't have very much time either. The fact is that I am being held captive, but I want you to promise that you won't tell anyone, especially the police. If you do, I may be killed."

Ikuo did not know what to say. For a moment he thought the other was joking, but then he noticed the tension in his voice. Gone was the bantering tone he had heard when they had met in the hotel lobby.

"Please swear that you will not tell anyone about it or I will hang up, but there is nobody else I can trust."

"Why? We hardly even know each other."

"I know. Apart from the fact that we have both dated the same girl, we have absolutely nothing in common. We are complete strangers, but you are suspected by the police of having committed a crime, and so you will be on your guard against them. It is only someone in your position who can help me."

Michitaro tried desperately to convince Ikuo of his position, but Ikuo could not really grasp that the other was actually being held captive. He just stood holding the phone and listening blankly.

"Please swear that you will not tell the police. My captors are listening to everything we're saying. I won't cause you any problems, but please help me."

"All right, I will do as you say," he answered reluctantly. In his mind's eye, he saw not the suave insurance executive, but a small boy with a soup-bowl haircut.

"Thank you very much. I'm sure I will be able to pay you back when I'm free—if I get out of this alive, that is.

At least, I think I will be able to prove it was not you who set fire to the house where the woman kept the lion."

The voice on the other end of the line became choked with emotion, but Ikuo remained silent.

"Next time I call, I want you to go to my mother's and collect the insurance money that the company will pay. It is the money due for the policy on the lion I mentioned the other day. A beneficiary has turned up, but the company does not want to pay. There is a lot of dispute about it, but I am sure my mother will be able to sort it out. I may not be able to call you myself next time, but if you get a call from someone calling herself 'The Firegirl,' I want you to do whatever she says. Have you got that? 'The Firegirl.' My life depends on it. I won't be able to talk so long next time, as they're scared you might have the call traced, but remember, 'The Firegirl.' "

It sounded as if he was pulled away from the phone, and then the line suddenly went dead.

"Who was it from?" his chief asked, seeing him standing there clutching the receiver to his chest without replacing it.

He wondered if the police already knew about the kidnapping. There had not been anything about it on the news. After a few moments' hesitation, he shook his head and replied, "It was just an old friend who suddenly telephoned me out of the blue."

As he spoke, he realized that he was indeed speaking the truth. He wondered why Michitaro should have called him for help. Surely he could not have remembered him. He realized that they must have been fated to meet again.

He waited impatiently for his duty to end and then went

out into the evening streets. He went to a coffee bar with a telephone in it and called the Fire Chief's daughter.

"Yes, he called me and insisted that I tell him your work number. Has anything happened? He told me he wouldn't be able to see me for some time, and when I called his house his mother was very cold toward me. She sounded as if she resented my call and just said that he was out. She refused to put me through to him."

She began to sob and Ikuo realized that she must have fallen for Michitaro. He had not felt particularly attracted toward her himself, but the thought that she had chosen another man made him feel strangely lonely.

"I'll get in touch as soon as I find out anything," he said. "When I do, I would appreciate it if you would come and meet me. If you are out, I will leave a message in his name and tell you where to come."

Next he dialed Michitaro's home number. Assuming the call might take some time, he dug into his pockets for some more change. As he did so, he looked around the coffee bar and noticed a well-dressed young man sitting in a corner reading a magazine. He seemed to be paying not the slightest attention to him, but Ikuo recognized him as being the man he had seen at the library when he had been checking through the old newspapers. Although the other man had given him a friendly look at the library, he was now acting with the affected unconcern that made it obvious that he was following him.

The telephone rang three times before it was answered.

"Hello, is this the Matsubara home? May I speak to Michitaro, please?"

"Who is this speaking?"

Ikuo hesitated for a moment, wondering whether he should give his name or not.

"I am a childhood friend of his. I have some urgent business with him."

"I am afraid he is out at the moment, but if you would like to leave a message . . ."

"Is this his mother speaking?"

He was suddenly overwhelmed by a feeling of nostalgia. He could remember standing outside Michitaro's house calling him, and the icy look his mother would give him when she let him into the house. Sometimes, however, she had treated them to toasted hotcakes, dripping with honey.

"Yes it is. Now what is your business?"

She sounded very cautious and more than a little irritable.

"Michitaro is out, is he? How long has he been away? It is very important that you answer me."

This time it was Ikuo who sounded very tense, but she did not answer him.

"He has been kidnapped, hasn't he? How long? It is important that you answer me if you want to save him."

There was a sharp intake on the other end of the line.

"If you are really my son's friend, why won't you tell me your name?" she pleaded, sounding like a mother for the first time.

"I have my reasons for not being able to give you my name, but I think I will be able to help your son. One thing I must get clear, however. Have you managed to get the money ready? The sum that the lion was insured for."

If he was to deliver the money, he wanted to make sure that all the preparations had been made.

135

solely to deal with cases like this. They are the enemies of the people, and someone like you, heir to a major insurance company, is bound to know about them."

"I am not heir to the company. I do not even hold an important post. The only reason they gave me the job I have was out of deference to my grandmother, who is still a major shareholder. But what is all this talk of an organization to kill people who defraud insurance companies? I have never heard anything so ridiculous in my life! Who are you? What do you want? If you are only after a ransom, there is no need to hurt me like this!"

His cheek hurt so much that he lost his temper and became quite aggressive toward them.

"As the grandson of the founder of one of the largest insurance companies in the world, you make a perfect example for others like you. Even if you know nothing about the fire personally, you still deserve everything you get. We represent all the little people that your company has been robbing for all these years.

"If you tell us the truth, however, we are willing to let you go. We won't even insist on getting your ransom. Now what do you say. Who was responsible for the fire that killed the woman and her lion? While you are at it, you had better tell us about all those other fires. Why did they always involve cardboard boxes? Why were there always a pile of burned matches left behind? What was their meaning? This is the last time we are going to ask. If you don't answer, we will continue to strike you every three minutes until you don't have an inch of skin left on your body."

There were two of them, and while one was doing the

talking the other was getting his next instrument ready to continue the torture.

"Don't think you can frighten me," Michitaro muttered. "I'd die before I told you anything. . . ."

The pain blossomed in his right cheek, but his interrogator did not say a word. It seemed like an age before the next blow fell, and, while he waited, the events of his past floated by his eyes like snapshots in an album. The memory of the time when he was five came back with remarkable clarity. Even now, he could see Ikuo in his blue shorts and with a scar on his left leg, as he climbed the stairs to the second floor. He had grabbed Ikuo's leg, but Ikuo had kicked him away and gone on upstairs.

He did not follow. His father was upstairs and he had been told that he was *never* to go up to the second floor on his own, and he always did what his mother told him. Ikuo was from another family, and he was not aware that it was forbidden, which was why he had gone upstairs. He had seen something up there, something that had made him turn white and tremble violently, but what could it have been? No, there was no need to ask, he knew what it was. After twenty-six years, in the midst of pain and fear, he could see Ikuo's face as clearly as if he were standing before him now, and he knew what he had seen. For a moment the pain seemed to subside, and he was filled with a feeling of warmth. He stretched out his hand toward the other.

"Hey, Ikuo, I've seen you recently!"

Yes, that fireman who was the suspect in the arson cases, surely that was the face of the grown-up Ikuo. Suddenly he wanted to see him again and ask him what he had seen when he had gone up to the second floor.

Just then the pain spread out from his right cheek, and it was so violent that the thread of his memory was broken. With the fresh pain, he was filled with despondency. He realized that the fireman could not really be the Ikuo of his youth. The fact that he was a fireman and also a suspect in the arson case had confused him. But the fireman's name was also Ikuo, and why had he felt so comfortable with him? The only explanation could be that he was the same Ikuo from his youth, but why had he not realized until now?

He raised his head. His right hand and both legs were bound to the chair.

"It was me! I set fire to the boxes outside the house where the lion was kept. I am responsible for all those fires. I enjoy lighting fires. I have enjoyed it since I was a child!"

This time they hit him even though he was still talking, and they sounded angry.

"That's the kind of thing we hate most of all. Trying to take the blame on yourself like that is just the kind of thing we should expect from a bourgeois fool like you. If you want to be a witness to the crimes your company has committed, O.K., but don't come out with that kind of rubbish again."

Hearing this, Michitaro suddenly broke into laughter. He had half suspected that his captors were really policemen pretending to be a leftist group and interrogating him to make him admit to lighting the fire. Now that he knew they were not police, the tension left him, and he found he was even able to grab a few moments' sleep during the torture.

4　*The Detective*

The Chief Inspector and Ryosaku looked through a two-way mirror into the interrogation room and saw Ikuo sitting in a chair still wearing handcuffs. His chin was thrust out aggressively, and he was obviously exercising his right to remain silent.

"We cannot keep him here forever, you know, and we can't charge him or the press will get wind of the kidnapping."

"But we've got a news blackout, haven't we?" Ryosaku asked conversationally, looking up at his superior's lined face. He was in a much easier position than the older man. He did not have to worry about the press or the political repercussions. The only thing that worried him was that he and the fireman shared the same lover.

"Yes, we've got a news blackout on this case, but if they find out that the fireman is involved, they won't be able to resist it. We have already had one reporter sniffing around here. Apparently he knows the suspect and intends to write a feature story about the case."

The Inspector made a bitter face. It had been his idea not to arrest the fireman, just to keep him under surveillance. It looked as if he wouldn't get his chance to act in an unpolicemanlike way after all.

"But I have been keeping him under constant surveillance, and I'd say that it would have been impossible for him to be one of the kidnappers," Ryosaku said to put his superior's mind at rest.

"I agree. We should not have arrested him like that after we traced the call. It is just unfortunate that there happened to be a couple of uniformed officers in a car nearby at the time."

"I was even closer. I was just sitting there like an idiot while he phoned the victim's mother. He made another call just before he made that one, which could either mean that he was contacting the kidnappers or . . ."

"Or what? You don't have to keep me in suspense, you know." The Inspector glared at him.

"He could have telephoned someone to find out the victim's home number."

"I hope you are not going to suggest that he rang Information, are you?"

"No, I meant the victim's girlfriend."

"You mean you know who she might be?" The Inspector's expression softened.

"Yes, the victim met the fireman once in the lobby of a hotel. It was quite accidental. The victim was there with his girl when they bumped into Onda. It was the girl who introduced them, and it turned out that she was the daughter of the Fire Chief. She had dated Onda a few times in the past, which explains how she knew him."

"Did you check up on her then?"

"Yes, sir."

Ryosaku hoped that he would not have to report on Chieko, too, before the case was finished.

"I think we will have to let him go. We must pretend we don't know anything about the kidnapping."

"But how do we explain our tracing his call?"

"If he doesn't say anything, neither will we. The victim's

family is acting as if nothing has happened, so if nobody says anything stupid, we should be all right."

"May I speak to him, sir? He knows my face now, so there is no need for me to pretend he doesn't."

The Chief Inspector looked thoughtful for a few moments before he spoke.

"I don't see why not. You'll have to talk about it sooner or later."

His tone seemed to suggest a double meaning, but Ryosaku did not notice. He walked tensely into the interrogation room and changed places with the detective there.

"I spoke to the Fire Chief's daughter about your connection with Michitaro. She says that you both dated her. She's a nice, bright girl. She'd make a good wife, you know."

Ikuo turned toward him, a look of surprise on his face.

"She says that you asked her for his telephone number. What did you say to his mother?"

Ikuo did not reply. There did not seem to be any point. He knew the police had been listening, so why bother to repeat what they already knew?

"Do you know where he is? You don't have to worry. I was following you when he disappeared, so I know you had nothing to do with his kidnapping. You were out jogging in your new jogging shoes when it happened."

Ikuo still did not answer. Ryosaku turned his chair around and sat astride it with his hands resting on the top of the backrest.

"You don't have to think of me as a policeman. I don't want you to make a statement or anything. You just want to help him, the same as me, so why don't we work together on it? You only want to send him back to his girl, don't you? By the way, did he phone you first?" He spoke as if they were old friends.

Ikuo answered at last, staring Ryosaku straight in the eye. "Yes, he rang me at work. He got the number from the girl."

"What did he say?"

"There was some money outstanding on an insurance policy that had to be paid. He said that his mother would get the money ready, and he asked me to pick it up, that's all. He said the money was for the lion that died in the fire, and he asked me to deliver it because I'm already involved in the case to a certain extent."

He spoke carefully, but Ryosaku shook his head.

"I don't think you're telling me everything, are you? You have known each other longer than that. You were childhood friends."

He rested his chin on the back of the chair and stared at Ikuo.

Ikuo returned his gaze.

"No, he knows nothing about that. He only called me because he thinks I am the arsonist who started the fires. He thought I would be the last person to go to the police after I had heard his story."

"I see. Well, in that case, we know nothing at all. We will let you go at once, and, although I will stick close to you, I will make it appear that I am just watching you in connection with the arson cases. But I will really be there to help you, and if anything happens, I want you to get in touch with me immediately. You understand, we aren't forcing you to do anything. We just want to help."

Ikuo did not reply, but he looked very worried.

"I just want you to tell me when they get in touch with you. Are they going to call you at your apartment?"

"He did not say anything about how he was going to get in touch next. I don't think he is free to decide. The moment he tried to mention the call being traced, the line suddenly went dead."

"When they get in touch with you next, it would be best if you kept quiet about being arrested today. If they should mention it, just say that we asked you in to pick up your license." He undid the handcuffs. "Please don't think badly about this. We only wanted to have a chat with you, but there are some people here who get a kick out of throwing their weight around."

Ikuo did not reply but rubbed his wrists moodily.

"Are you sure that he does not realize you were childhood friends?" Ryosaku asked when they were sitting in the back of a squad car together on the way back to Ikuo's apartment.

"Yes. He told me about the fire he had experienced as a child and it set me thinking, so I went to the library and checked on the old papers—as you well know."

Ikuo spoke with a trace of sarcasm, keeping his eyes on the back of the uniformed driver's head.

"Oh yes, those articles were very interesting. They made quite a fuss at the time, didn't they. It was not just a case of arson. His father's body was found in the wreckage of the house, and there was even some talk of murder."

"Yes, I wish I could remember it a bit clearer, but I can't. Can you remember when you were five?"

Ryosaku shook his head.

"It's difficult to remember things that happened when you were that young, isn't it? I suppose if you thought about it hard enough it might come back to you, but I cannot even remember when my mother died."

"Neither can I."

Ikuo was only making conversation, but it surprised Ryosaku, and he hurriedly changed the subject. He did not think this was the time to tell Ikuo that he was the other child from those distant days.

"Anyway, I will be nearby in an unmarked car, so if anything happens, let me know straight away. If they contact you, hang a woman's bra or a pair of panties or something outside your window, and I will be round in a flash. I'm counting on you, my fireman."

The moment those last two words left his lips, he knew that he had overdone it. He remembered the nurse telling him that "my fireman," in English, was her pet name for Ikuo when they were together. Now it had just slipped out. Ikuo turned as he got out of the car and gave him a long look filled with suspicion and sadness.

5   The Fireman

Ikuo reached out sleepily for the phone, and it was a few moments before he recognized Michitaro's voice.

"Ikuo?" Michitaro sounded almost like a child, and the voice showed the strain he was under.

"Yes, it's me. I have been in touch with your mother for you."

"Thanks a lot. I'm sorry to keep asking you all this, but could you work with my girl from now on. She's on her way over to pick you up. Are you being followed?"

"I don't know," Ikuo said, picking his words carefully. The line went dead.

Ikuo got up and was still getting dressed when he heard a car pull up outside. The Fire Chief's daughter hurried up to his room.

"Michitaro is behaving very strangely. He told me not to ask any questions but to come and pick you up. There is a taxi waiting downstairs."

She was obviously in love with Michitaro and looked somehow sexier than when he had first met her. There had been a chance she would have married him, and he regretted now that he had not paid more attention to her. But this was not the time to think about such things.

"What did he say?"

"He told me to take you to a hotel in Yokohama. I have been there before, so I know where it is."

"Is that where you two always go?"

"No, we have only been once."

She answered without hesitation, and it came as a bit of a blow to his pride. He didn't think she was the type to indulge in premarital sex.

He followed her down to the waiting taxi, and she directed it to take them to a high-rise hotel in the Shinjuku area. They got out, and she paid more than was shown on the meter and asked the driver to wait fifteen minutes for them.

"That's what he told me to do, and he said that whatever we did, we weren't to look back."

She took his arm, and he was glad he had changed into a suit and a clean shirt.

"Are we going to meet him in a bar here or something?"

147

"No, this hotel has another exit, and there's a long-distance taxi stand there for people who want to go to the airport. We are to pick up another taxi there."

She guided them briskly all the way around the hotel before pushing him into a long-distance taxi.

"There is an expressway interchange up ahead. I was told to go up onto the expressway and to make sure we weren't being followed."

She kept her hand on his arm as she peered around to watch the cars behind them.

"It's all right, there is no one following," she whispered in his ear, and he realized that the kidnappers had given this a lot of thought before they gave her their instructions.

"Did he tell you what had happened?"

"No, he told me not to ask any questions, but I could tell that he is in great danger and that I had to do everything I could in order to save him."

Ikuo reflected that Michitaro and the Fire Chief's daughter would make a good couple, providing Michitaro came out of this unharmed.

She had the taxi stop outside a well-known hotel next to Yamanote Park and paid double the fare.

"He said that after the taxi had driven off, we should walk in the park for about five minutes."

They strolled around the park arm in arm like lovers, and every so often they would stop and embrace, but instead of kissing, she told him to look around to see if they were being followed. Ikuo felt sure that even if they had been followed, their tail must have been thrown off the scent by now, and he could not help feel a twinge of regret about having let the detective down. He should at least have hung a handkerchief outside his window for him.

They walked out the other side of the park, and this time she led him into a modern hotel where a room had already been reserved in her name.

"We are to wait for him to contact us here, but in the meantime, how about a beer?" she said, opening the fridge in their room.

Ikuo had just lifted his glass to his lips when the phone rang. It was Michitaro, and he still sounded exhausted.

"Ikuo, I knew I could rely on you to help me." He seemed to be almost chanting the words, and Ikuo realized that Michitaro might have remembered their childhood days after all.

"I'm not going to waste words. I am going to tell you what to do with the insurance money when you get it from my mother, but I don't want you to take notes. I want you to memorize my instructions."

He avoided using the term *ransom money*.

"O.K., I won't take any notes then!"

"When you get the money from my mother, I want you to put it in a duffel bag, a strong, waterproof, canvas one, and then throw it off the fire engine. The amount should be the same as was due for the lion, and it should be in large-denomination American bills. The company should be able to arrange that."

He broke off into a painful fit of coughing.

"Hey! Are you all right?"

The girl had been standing in the corner of the room, her hands clasped worriedly in front of her. Hearing Ikuo call out, she crossed the room toward him, but he waved her away. If there was any danger involved, he wanted to keep her out of it.

"I'm O.K. At two o'clock in the morning, two nights from now, when you are on night shift, there will be a fire in your area. When you go out on the fire engine, I want you to take the bag with you. You will be contacted at one minute to two and told where you are to drop the bag. I know it is probably forbidden for you to take private calls when you are on duty, but if you refuse, I will be killed. Even if you don't refuse, I will probably be—"

The line suddenly went dead, and Ikuo knocked back the beer he had in his glass in one gulp. The phone soon rang again.

"I forgot to mention that should your duty be changed, you are to hang a woman's bra outside your window. I know that it is in rather bad taste, but that's what they want."

He did his best to sound relaxed and even tried to make a joke of his instructions, saying that Ikuo should be pleased he did not have to find a pair of panties.

"Are you sure you don't want to talk to the girl?"

Michitaro was silent for a moment.

"Thank her for me. Oh yes, one more thing. I want you both to stay in your room until morning. You're not on duty tomorrow, so I want you both to stay there until ten o'clock in the morning and then leave as if you are lovers, exhausted after a night of sex. I won't mind if you really are exhausted."

He added this last remark as a joke, in an effort to cheer himself up.

"Don't worry, we won't be wasting our energy. We need

all our strength if we are going to help you. May I tell your mother that you are fine? She must be worried about you, and she has to arrange for the money."

"O.K., but leave it until tomorrow, after you have left the hotel. Thanks again for everything."

The phone was hung up quietly, and it was obvious that Michitaro had done it of his own volition this time. After the line had gone dead, Ikuo realized that he did not have anything to do until morning. He went to the fridge and took out another beer, a small bottle of whiskey, some saké, and a bag of nuts.

He was going to need some alcohol if he was to sleep tonight, otherwise he would not be able to remain in the room. He could already feel himself attracted to the beautiful young woman who was with him, and it was all he could do to control his emotions. As she buried her head in his chest, however, she did not seem to realize how he felt.

"Will he be all right?" she asked. "Will he come home alive? You often hear of kidnappers who kill their victims after they have received the ransom. He is not a child; he is an adult, and he must have seen their faces."

"That's the problem."

He felt the same uncertainty and hugged her to him. They fell to the bed, and, contrary to his good resolutions, their lips met, his hand slipping down toward her thighs . . .

6 *The Arsonist*

Michitaro pointed toward the telephone. In the midst of his pain and exhaustion, he felt that he wanted to talk to

Ikuo one more time. He might never have the chance again.

He spoke to the man who was sitting on the other bed and unwrapping another strip of chewing gum. "I want him to commit himself to helping me. We used to be friends, you know, when we were five."

The man had a gun fitted with a silencer thrust into his belt, and he behaved naturally about it, as though he was quite at home with guns. All of Michitaro's captors were the same. There was nothing theatrical or false about them. They were totally used to living with weapons. They seemed to be more than just kidnappers or killers; they seemed to have a sense of mission, and that gave meaning to their lives.

"I haven't got the authority to make a decision," the man said calmly, as he put the chewing gum in his mouth.

"But there's something I forgot to tell him. I've got to make quite sure he is on my side, or he might go to the police."

Michitaro looked the man in the eye. This was not one of the men who had tortured him. The group appeared to consist of at least four people, and there was a strict chain of command.

"O.K., but only for five minutes."

"Five minutes is not enough. I've got to make him remember when we were five years old. That's twenty-six years ago."

He clutched his left side. The blow he had received there had hurt much longer than the others, and he thought he might have a cracked rib.

The man picked up the phone and dialed a number. He spoke for about a minute in a language that Michitaro could not understand, but he recognized it as being Arabic.

"O.K., but don't let him know you are calling him from the same hotel."

The man dialed an internal number and spat out his chewing gum. When the phone was answered, he affected the tired voice of a night porter.

"I have a call for you, sir."

He gave the phone to Michitaro.

"There is something I forgot to ask you. It is a personal thing."

Ikuo sounded as if he had just been roused from a deep sleep and responded in a thick voice. Not only did Michitaro feel jealous that Ikuo could sleep at a time like this, but he felt as if he had been forgotten.

The rooms they occupied were one on top of the other. Thus they were only a few feet apart.

"I want you to go to the safe on the floor of my garage and pick up the things you find there. There is a rubber bag filled with gasoline, a rope lighter, and, although you may find this a little strange, several bundles of burned matches tied with rubber bands. I would like you to put them in the bag with the money when you drop it off the fire truck, although this is an entirely personal request. Are you listening?"

"Yes, I'm listening. I am to pick up a bag of gasoline, a lighter, and bundles of burned matches."

Ikuo was still half asleep, and he just repeated what he had heard parrot fashion. He did not seem to grasp the importance of it.

"Those dead matches are the same ones we used when we played as children," Michitaro whispered nostalgically.

His guard walked over to the bedside table where the telephone sat. For a moment, Michitaro thought the guard was going to cut him off, but he only picked up the cigarettes he had left there.

"What did you just say?" Ikuo asked, suddenly waking up, his voice becoming tense.

"I said they are the same matches that we used when we played as children."

"Why do you still have them?"

"Didn't you know that my mother is very keen on education? She used to show me those dead matches every day and ask me if I could tell her the connection between them and my father's death. She always wept as she asked me, and the matches are soaked with her tears."

Ikuo's breathing came to him over the line. It was not just because they were so close to each other and the line was clear, rather, Michitaro had torn aside the veil of the last twenty-six years and left Ikuo to confront their past in the dark hotel room.

Ikuo was silent as he thought over the meaning of what he had heard. Then he said in a clear voice, "Is that why you always scattered burned matches around when you set fire to the boxes?"

"Yes, that's part of the reason, but it's not all." His shoulders slumped, and he did not know how to continue. He called out the other's name, and it was the cry of a lost child calling for a friend. "Ikuo! I always knew we would meet. I could feel you near me whenever I went out to light the fires."

Ikuo did not reply, and Michitaro wondered if he was angry. After all, he had let him take the blame for the fires.

"When we met in the hotel, did you realize who I was?" asked Ikuo, at last. "Is that why you spoke about the fire?"

"No, I had no idea. I thought you were just some fool of a fireman who was so eager to get the credit for capturing me that you ended up getting blamed for the fires yourself. After I was kidnapped, I kept repeating your name and it suddenly came back to me. To be quite honest, I still cannot remember what you looked like then."

"I can remember you." Whether it was intentional or not, Ikuo's voice had become very cold.

"My mother remembers us always playing with fire in those days, and no matter how often she scolded us we wouldn't stop. It went on for about a fortnight, and on one occasion a fire had started to catch but she managed to put it out. She used to confiscate the matches from us, but you or the other boy would always bring some more from your houses. In those days, it was in vogue to advertise on the side of matchboxes, and everybody collected them."

He merely repeated what his mother had told him over the years, but for some reason he no longer considered it important to talk to Ikuo, and he even began to feel drowsy.

"Do you remember what happened that day?" Ikuo asked.

"No, I don't. I only know what my mother told me. She was out when the fire started, and by the time she got home, it was too late. When she saw what had happened, she panicked and forgot all about my father sleeping on the second floor. She didn't manage to save anything from the house at all."

He spoke as if he were reciting a fairy tale, and as his mother must have told him the story so many times, he had forgotten what the truth was.

"So she didn't save anything from the house?"

"Well, she did get the dead matches. Apparently we had left piles of them scattered around the house, and she collected them all and put them in her bag."

"Why?"

"Obviously so nobody would ever know that it was us who had caused the fire. She acted like a typical mother, but it didn't occur to her that after ten minutes or so the evidence would have been destroyed anyway."

"But don't you remember anything yourself? I don't mean something that you heard from someone else, I mean a real memory. Just before the fire started, we were playing hide-and-seek. The other boy was 'it,' and we decided to hide on the second floor. I went first, but you said that we should not go upstairs and grabbed me by the ankle." For some reason, Ikuo felt that Michitaro did not want to hear what happened afterward. "When you grabbed me, I kicked you away and ran upstairs."

Hearing this, Michitaro realized that Ikuo had remembered what had happened. He thought of asking what he had seen, but it would not help him now even if he knew, so he did not bother and put the phone down.

PART
SIX

1 *The Detective*

Ryosaku looked at his watch as he walked through the temple gate. Michitaro's mother would be finished copying the sutras in another five minutes. The fact that she was able to make use of the main hall of the temple whenever she liked showed just how deep her connection with the temple was.

Ryosaku was dressed in a safari suit. Carrying a small bunch of roses in his right hand, he walked among the stone Buddhas until he came to the small statue of the poodle, which was buried up to a third of its height in the earth.

"It suddenly appeared again three days ago without anyone getting permission from me, so I thought I had better let you know," the chief priest said. He had noticed the detective enter through the gate and had come over to see him.

"I have been very busy on the case these last few days," Ryosaku said by way of apology for not having come right away.

"I daresay, one reads so many terrible things in the papers, it must be the end of the world. Everybody seems to be too busy to rest these days. Oh, yes. The person you were asking about is in the main hall at the moment making her devotions. I haven't said anything about your being here."

"Thank you. When she is finished, could you tell her that I am here?"

No matter how long Ryosaku stared at the statue, it looked more like a real lion than a poodle. He stood looking at it in silence until he heard the sound of her high heels approaching from behind.

"Are you from the police?"

"Yes, I am, but I would like to talk to you about a personal matter. You must be very upset about Michitaro's disappearance."

"Yes, I just hope he comes home safely as soon as possible. In the meantime, I spend my time in the temple here, praying."

She did not show her fear, and Ryosaku saw that she had hardly changed since he was a child. It was he who had changed. Twenty-six years ago he had been a mere child and had felt overpowered and terrified of her. She had taken his hand firmly and said, "If it was you who lit the fire, tell me now, otherwise . . ." She had told him that the devil would tear out his tongue and that the stone Buddhas would come to his room every night and threaten him until he confessed. It had been terrible to frighten a young child that way, but even though he had been terrified, he had not confessed to starting the fire.

"Does this statue represent Michitaro's poodle?"

"Yes, that is correct."

"It was placed here three days ago. Do you know anything about that?"

"No, I don't," she said, shaking her head. Ryosaku had not expected otherwise.

"Was it you who ordered this statue in memory of your son's poodle?"

This time she nodded, reluctantly. "Who told you that Michitaro kept a poodle?"

"He did himself. I met him when I was investigating the insurance policy. By the way, how did the dog die?"

"He died in a fire. That's why I had the memorial erected in this temple. He had kept that dog for thirteen years and thought of it as a brother, but he had no interest in religion, so it was I who arranged to have the statue made. He didn't know anything about it."

"Was this before the fire in which the lion died?"

"Yes, the dog died a long time before that, and it was about the same time that I had the statue made and erected on this spot."

"Did you know that soon after the lion died, the statue was removed from this spot?"

"No, I had no idea. After all, it was only a dog, and I forgot all about it after the statue was completed."

"So you have no idea who might have removed it?"

"Well, actually I do, but I don't think I can tell you at the moment."

She gripped the top of her crocodile-skin handbag and gazed resolutely ahead. Ryosaku decided to change the line of his questioning.

"Could you tell me a bit more about the circumstances concerning the dog's death?"

"Well, I was out at the time, and I returned home to find the dog already dead. According to my son, the dog had knocked over a can of paint and was covered in it. As you know, it was a long-haired dog, and in order to remove the paint my son used benzene, but the dog managed to escape, and when it ran by the gas stove it caught fire. Apparently it was all over in a moment, and there was nothing Michitaro could do to save it."

"Do you use gas stoves in your house?"

"Only in the garage basement. My son is interested in do-it-yourself projects, and he keeps all kinds of paints and tools and things down there. It was a great shock to him, and that's why I decided to have the statue erected here."

"It must have been a special shock for him, having lost his father in a fire, too."

"It would appear that there is nothing the police don't know."

"I was only a child at the time, but I remember all the talk about it in the papers."

"Yes, the children were playing with matches, and the house caught fire. The house was completely destroyed, and my husband didn't manage to escape."

She seemed not to realize who he was. He raised his eyes from the statue and looked at the other statues.

"It was not only your husband that died, was it? Didn't a dog die that time, too?"

He tried not to change his tone as he asked. She did not answer straight away. She seemed to be immersed in her own memories for a moment and to have forgotten all about his presence.

"Yes, it was my husband's dog. Its body was found next

160

to my husband's, and everyone praised it for being so loyal. It was a Scottish terrier."

Ryosaku had tried to visualize the dog, but he had absolutely no recollection of it at all. All he knew about it was what he had read in the newspapers in the library.

"Are you against the construction of the condominiums? Do you want to preserve these statues?"

"No, that has nothing to do with me," she said.

He stood looking at the flowers he had left at the feet of the statue. He had an idea that was so stupid he hesitated to put it into words, but he could not think of anything else to say, so he asked her anyway. If nothing else, it would be a way of finishing off the interview.

"Twenty-six years ago, didn't you erect a statue to the dog that died with your husband in the fire?"

"No, I didn't. I had more on my mind than worrying about a dog. My husband was dead, and I was left to raise a five-year-old son on my own."

"Yes, I see." It had been a stupid question.

He felt a shiver run up his spine. When she had dragged him here as a boy in an effort to make him admit lighting the fire, it was not a statue of Buddha that she made him stand in front of, but a statue of a dog. The memory suddenly came back to him as if it were yesterday.

"Why are the police so interested in the statue of a poodle, anyway?" she asked.

"I am more interested in a personal capacity than an official one."

"Why?"

She gazed at him intently for a short while, then turned and started to walk away. After she had gone about three steps, she turned and said, "I see, you were one of those children, weren't you? What was your name? Ryosaku, wasn't it?" Her face softened slightly. "I have been told to leave my son's ransom by that statue, so it would be a great help if you were not to leave flowers there. They might draw people's attention to the spot."

So saying, she turned and walked briskly away toward the temple gate.

2   The Fireman

Ikuo went to Michitaro's house, and even though he had been expecting something grand, he was amazed by the opulence of the building. It was surrounded by a high wall, and there were several large trees in the garden. It showed just how much money his father had left them when he died.

Living in a house like this, it is not surprising that he got kidnapped, Ikuo thought to himself as he went up to the door. He guessed that the police were keeping the place under surveillance, but there was no sign of them anywhere.

He gave his name on the intercom, and the iron gate opened by remote control. Michitaro's mother came to the door to greet him, and although she showed a few traces of the strain she was under, she was still as beautiful as ever. Ikuo was amazed to find that even after twenty-six years he could still recognize her as the mother of his childhood friend.

"I have no way of knowing if you are really doing this for my son," she said.

"Certainly you must have heard something from him yourself," he replied. "I only have to collect the insurance money and hand it over to the kidnappers. After that, Michitaro should be released."

As he sat in a chair in the vestibule, Ikuo realized what a dangerous gamble he was taking. He was walking on thin ice, and he had no idea when it might break and the police come in to arrest him. As it was, Michitaro's mother did not seem very keen to give him the money.

"As you say, I had a call from Michitaro telling me to give you the money. But I also had a letter telling me to leave the money somewhere else. I do not think the letter was a hoax because nobody but the kidnappers and the police know that Michitaro has been kidnapped, and the place they stipulated made sense."

"O.K., I will be going then."

He started to get up.

"Wait a minute. Has my son really been kidnapped? How are you to hand the money over to his kidnappers?"

"I cannot answer that. I know nothing about the gang that kidnapped your son. I just believed him when he asked me to help, and I am doing as he said."

Their conversation did not seem to be getting anywhere, and he found himself becoming irritated.

"Are you sure that my son is not just pretending to have been kidnapped?"

"There is always that chance," he replied blandly.

"What is your relationship with him?"

"We are old friends."

Even though it was true, it seemed strange for him to put it into words.

"I feel as if I have met you before."

"You probably saw my picture in the papers after that lion died in the fire. It was my license and I.D. they found in the lion's stomach."

"Yes, I know, but I don't mean recently. I mean a long time ago. You were at nursery school together, weren't you? How did my son get in touch with you again?"

"Yes, that's right, we used to know each other, but our meeting again was a complete accident."

He found this conversation becoming very tedious. He had had no intention of bringing up the subject of their youth.

"So I was right then. What a strange few days this has been. You know, I met the other boy whom you played with in those days, too. You have all grown up to be fine young men."

She gave a sigh, but Ikuo remained silent. For some reason, he could not feel nostalgic about the past.

"I don't know why Michitaro asked me to do this, but he said that his life depended on it, so I agreed to help."

"Well, now that I know who you are, I see that I have no option but to do as you say. But I still think Michitaro is faking it."

She kept repeating this as if she were trying to convince herself that there was really nothing to worry about. She produced a small satchel filled with the money.

"This is as much as the company was able to get in American dollars."

"I don't want to see the contents. It could be old newspapers for all I care. That's your problem, not mine. But there is one more thing I must ask. Would you show me the garage basement, please?"

Ikuo felt that this was important. Michitaro had wanted him to go on his own, but he wanted the mother to go with him.

"What do you want in the garage?"

"Michitaro asked me to pick something up for him."

"And what was that?"

"Some burned matches, a rope lighter, and a rubber bag of gasoline."

"Are those things in the garage basement?" she asked, feigning astonishment.

"Michitaro said they were and asked me to take them to him," he said, standing up and showing as little emotion as possible. He avoided looking her in the eye, but he could tell that his request had come as a shock to her.

"But there are some policemen in the garage. They have a radio in there, and I have not told them I was going to give you the money to deliver."

Ikuo thought for a few seconds before answering. "In that case, would you please go and get the items I just mentioned and bring them here without attracting their suspicion? He said they were kept in a hidden safe in the basement." He realized that it would be best if she was to pick them up. What he feared more than anything else was that, if he was caught carrying the arsonist's tools, he might be accused of being the arsonist himself.

She returned after about twenty minutes.

"I wonder how long he has kept these things down there. Although they were kept in a secret safe, the key was left in the door, and the dial was taped so it would not move. But anyone could have opened it."

Ikuo took the red toolbox from her and looked inside. Everything was there, just as he had said: the lighter, the bag of gasoline, and the burned matches. There must have been at least three hundred matches all tied with rubber bands in bunches of twenty or thirty.

"What are all those things for?"

"They're for committing arson."

"Are you suggesting that my son is an arsonist?"

"I don't know, but in all the recent fires, the arsonist has left a large number of burned matches scattered around, much more than he would need to start the fire. They were necessary for the ceremony he likes to perform."

"Why?"

"I don't know, but the matchsticks were always wet. Maybe he was trying to hint at something."

"But what?" she asked persistently.

For a moment he thought of saying they were soaked with a mother's tears, but something stopped him, and instead he said that the arsonist had urinated on them.

"Anyway, I will deliver all these, but I don't know when your son will be released."

He picked up the bag of money and the red toolbox.

"Do you really think my son is an arsonist?"

"I don't know. All I do know is that I am suspected of being the arsonist, and the contents of this toolbox might prove my innocence. All the same, these matches don't look twenty-six years old to me. What do you think?"

"What is that supposed to mean?"

This time Ikuo met her gaze.

"Michitaro said these are the matches we used all those years ago when we were playing and started the fire. He said you managed to rescue them from the burning house before they were destroyed."

She did not deny or confirm what he said, but just moved her head slightly from left to right.

3 *The Arsonist*

Michitaro could hear the sound of a fire engine's siren in the distance, and he wondered what the time was. Since being kidnapped he had been without a watch, but he guessed that it was about five minutes past two in the morning.

He wondered where the fire was. He had always set his own fires at this time in the evening, and in those fire-starting days he would now be experiencing the fear and rapture of watching the fire spread from the boxes to the houses. He wondered why his kidnappers had chosen this particular time to set their fire. Was it merely because it was the dead of night, or was there some all-powerful God out there who had chosen this time to punish him for his sins?

He thought over everything he had done and wondered which of his crimes he was being punished for—or were they even crimes? Hadn't he been right to act as he did?

He heard another siren. This one passed close by, and there was no doubt that it was a fire engine. The sound that had once given him an almost sensual thrill now only served to heighten his fear.

There was nobody else left in the room. They had bound him hand and foot, gagged him with some adhesive tape over his mouth, and then left him all alone. He struggled to loosen the ropes, but it was no good. He had been trying for the last ten minutes, but they were as tight as ever.

He wondered if Ikuo would manage to hand over the money without any problems. The fire engine would have to slow down to turn right at the second set of lights after leaving the fire station, and, as it did so, Ikuo was to throw the bag of money into the dark parking lot next to a bank. That would be the first step toward his freedom, and, if his kidnappers kept their word, he would soon be a free man.

But his life would never be the same again. He had told the kidnappers and Ikuo all about his secret activities, so never again would he be able to flit through the night like a shadow, looking for boxes to feed his desire.

If Ikuo failed to give them the money, they would kill him. They had threatened to make an example of him, but he could not understand what he was to be an example of.

He thought of his father and of his mother who had had to raise him on her own. Then he thought of the omniscient person who had written him those secret letters. Until he had been kidnapped, he had refused to face the facts. He could not believe in anyone so all-knowing as to be able to make him pay for his crimes.

Another fire engine screamed past, and he wondered where the fire was. He also wondered where he was being kept. In a fit of frustration, he kicked out with his right foot, and it almost felt as if the knot loosened a little. He kicked with his left foot and twisted his wrists, and for the first time in his life he fought with all his strength against something that was trying to destroy him. Until now, he had always averted his eyes and directed his energies against something else.

Finally, his legs were free. He staggered to his feet and turned the knob of the door with his hands, which were still tied behind him. The door swung open. They had not locked it! He guessed that Ikuo must have succeeded in handing over the money and that he had been saved. He felt as if all the strength had left his body.

He was still naked, as he had been when he was first kidnapped. There was nothing in the pockets of the cape they had given him, and he realized how helpless he was without any money. He could not go straight to the police like this to give himself up. He had to see Ikuo first and talk to him. Ikuo had to have seen it.

Twenty-six years ago, he had grabbed Ikuo by the ankle on the stairs, but Ikuo had managed to break away and get to the second floor. He must have seen it. He had to meet Ikuo and learn what he had seen. That was all he could think of.

Leaving the room where he had been held captive and walking through the dark, he soon realized that he was in a deserted factory in the road behind the house where the woman with the lion had lived. It had once produced oil stoves, but it had closed down, and there was soon to be a large supermarket with a parking lot built on the spot. He had studied this area very carefully, as it was where he used to set his fires, so he managed to get his bearings quickly.

He came across a broken window and managed to use one of the shards of glass to cut through the rope binding his hands. He gingerly removed the tape from his mouth and realized that he was completely free at last. Outside the main gate of the factory, there was a phone booth, and he looked through the pockets of the cape again searching for some change, but there was none.

He looked inside the phone booth and could hardly believe his luck when he noticed a small woman's purse sitting on top of the directories. He opened it and saw that it contained several ten-yen coins and hundred-yen coins together with a folded thousand-yen note.

It was only fair that, after so much bad fortune, he should have a little luck. He dialed his home number, but despite the lateness of the hour the line was busy. Next he called Ikuo's apartment. He knew in the back of his mind that Ikuo was on duty and would not be at home, but he was not thinking logically. He wanted desperately to talk to Ikuo. All through his confinement, he had recited Ikuo's home number, and now he dialed it without hesitation.

When someone answered the phone, he immediately started to speak.

"Ikuo? It's me. Michitaro. There's something I have just got to know. What did you see? . . . that time when we were playing at my house . . . when we were five. We were playing hide-and-seek, and you started running upstairs. I grabbed your ankle, but you kicked me away and kept running. What did you see? My father was up there recovering from a cold, but what did you see? No, you don't have to answer. I know. I have known all the time. Someone told me. Someone couldn't just leave well enough alone, and they had to tell me. Just a minute . . . I'm in terrible pain. . . . After the beatings they gave me . . . I'm nearly done for."

He knelt down in the phone booth. He was shivering violently and felt as if he had a fever.

"I am O.K. now. It just hurts a bit. But I really do know what you saw. My father . . . my father was dead, wasn't he? How was he murdered? No, you don't have to answer that. It is enough that he was killed."

He started to cry. He could not stop himself; the sobs just seemed to force their way out through his throat.

Suddenly a woman's voice spoke coldly, and he realized that he had said something he should never have told another soul.

"This is Michitaro Matsubara, isn't it? Where are you? I will send someone to pick you up. Stay where you are."

He thought of putting the phone down without saying another word, but whom on earth had he phoned?

"Hello, where are you? Where are you calling from?"

He gave the name of the deserted factory where he had been held. The oil stoves it had produced when it had been in business were supposed to extinguish themselves automatically if they toppled over, but when he had tried it, the fire had spread and burned his pet poodle to death. He could not remember now why he had done it. What had it all been for, and why had he lied to his mother, telling her that the poodle had run too near a gas stove when it had benzene on its fur? He had spent his whole life since he was five making pointless experiments in order to deny the fact that his father had died in a fire.

He squatted down in the phone booth for about five minutes. The woman on the phone had said that a patrol car would arrive in two or three minutes, so he guessed that she must have been a policewoman.

Seeing the headlights of a car turn into the street, he stepped out of the phone booth. A major new trunk road had been built about ten yards away, so very few people had occasion to use this road so late at night.

The car had its high beams on, and when the driver saw him he slowed down for a moment, then suddenly accelerated. Michitaro was too exhausted to evade the car, and his body was thrown up into the air like a rag doll. Thankfully, he lost consciousness before he felt any pain.

4   The Detective

Ryosaku drank a cup of water from the water cooler in the waiting room before he settled back to wait for the nurse.

He sat looking at the hundred or so patients and relatives who were sitting quietly, waiting for their names to be called, and cast his mind back to the time when his wife had been a patient in this hospital. Losing his wife had been a terrible blow to him, and all the color seemed to go out of the world. Now his childhood friend, a man the same age as he, was also at death's door, but he did not feel so strongly about it. He reasoned that all men must die some time, and there was nothing he or anyone else could do about it.

"I am afraid the patient is still in no condition to talk."

He looked up and saw the nurse coming over to him. She spoke in a businesslike manner and seemed completely different from the passionate woman he knew in bed, but watching her as she marched confidently past the waiting people, he felt his pulse start to quicken. He realized he was very attracted to her both physically and mentally.

"That's O.K. I just came to see how he was. I wasn't involved in the kidnap case, so there's no need for me to talk to him. In fact, until someone is able to interview him, we don't even know if he really was kidnapped or not. Several of the men on the investigation are of the opinion that he faked the whole thing to get the money from his company."

He followed her up to a coffee shop on the roof of the building.

"Fate moves in mysterious ways, doesn't it? The first time I came here was when my wife was hospitalized, the next was when I was investigating a suspect in an arson case, and this time I am here to see the victim of a kidnapping. And every time, who should be there to greet me with a bright smile, like an angel in white? You."

"Are you being sarcastic?"

"No, I mean it. You are an extremely attractive woman, so much so that I can't stop thinking about you."

"I wish you wouldn't come here to chat with me like this when I am supposed to be working, but I know what you mean. I don't know if it is just coincidence or the hand of fate, but I sometimes feel that everything we do is preordained, and it almost makes me want to believe in the hand of God."

She put a lot of sugar in her coffee. Although she seemed to be quite lively, Ryosaku thought that she was probably really exhausted and that her body needed the sugar for energy.

"What's come over you? It's not like you to talk like that."

"Well, it's the grandmother of this patient. She is an old woman now, but I got to know her when I was working in the gynecological ward. She had uterine cancer and was in the hospital for about six months, but she is fine now. When the patient was admitted, she telephoned and hurried over, but she doesn't get on very well with her daughter-in-law. It was terrible. They just glared at each other in hatred and didn't say a word. She was such a kind old lady when she was in the hospital, always smiling, and I could hardly believe it was the same woman."

She spoke with passion, obviously eager to tell someone her story.

"Do you mean the wife of the late founder of the insurance company? She is still a large shareholder, isn't she?"

"Yes, she is very rich. When she left the hospital, she gave me a tip, but when I looked at the check, I couldn't believe my eyes. It was more than I earn in a year, and I was sure she had made a mistake. Did you know that she had disinherited her only son and then lost him in a tragic accident a short while later? When she is strict she is very strict, but when she is kind, she is embarrassingly so. I knew when I saw the money that it would only spoil me if I was to use it on myself, so I donated it to the building fund for the hospice."

"You are quite a special person," said Ryosaku.

He had never seen her in this light before. When they had been in bed together, she always seemed to avoid talking about herself, and this was the first time she had ever bared her soul to him.

"When she left the hospital, she asked me if I would leave the hospital and work for her as her private nurse. She said that if I was to stay with her until she died, she would leave me half of her fortune, but I turned her down. Now

I have to look after her grandson. I was on duty, so I had no choice, but it means that I will be meeting her and, if she offers me the job again, I don't know what I should do. I am not a saint, after all."

"Then why not accept her offer and look after her. She can't last much longer, and even after death duties, half of her fortune would be more than enough to keep you in luxury for the rest of your life."

"What a terrible thing to say. I was thinking of settling down and having your child. That's why I cannot make up my mind."

She sounded on the verge of tears, and Ryosaku hurriedly took back his words. He wanted to hug her to him, but instead, he just reached out and took her hand. It was as cold as ice.

"About the patient," she said in a strained voice, "they took him into the operating theater as soon as he was brought in, but before they did, he kept calling for Ikuo. I guessed straight away that he meant Ikuo Onda, so I listened to what he had to say. I was with him until morning, you know. You three were friends when you were young, so I will tell you what he said. But don't ask me to repeat it to anyone else, because I will refuse.

"He spoke about that time when you were five and his house caught on fire. He said that Ikuo had gone upstairs and he wanted to know what Ikuo had seen there. He knows now that his father did not die in the fire but had already been dead and that Ikuo had seen evidence of this. He kept asking Ikuo if it was true, and I had to make him calm down, so I took his hand and pretended that I was Ikuo. 'Yes,' I said, 'I saw your father. He had been strangled and was lying on his back on the floor, but I was scared and hurried downstairs again.' I kept repeating it to him, and, you know, I almost felt as if I could see a man lying murdered in his bedroom."

She put a handkerchief to her mouth and started to cry.

"Don't be silly, you're just tired. I was there when the fire started. I was only five, but I can remember quite clearly that we had been playing with matches. That was how the fire started. Nobody had been murdered upstairs."

He patted her gently on the back and helped her to her feet.

As he spoke, he remembered the scene quite vividly. The boys had all been striking matches and teasing Michitaro's pet beetle with the flames—or had that been another day?

"But he did see something. When Ikuo used to stay at my place, he kept having these terrible nightmares. He would cry out in his sleep about a man being killed, being strangled and lying there with foam on his lips. He was dreaming about something that he had seen when he was younger. I once asked him if he had seen something that frightened him when he was a child. His eyes went misty and he stared into space for a while. He wouldn't answer me, but I know now what it was."

"O.K., possibly he saw something, but even if there had been a murder, it was twenty-six years ago, and the statute of limitations on it has long since expired," he said irritably. "But how about your patient? Do you think he's going to be all right?"

"I don't think so. I think he will die. When they ran over him, they did so with the intention of killing him."

"But they had received their ransom money. Ikuo threw

it off the back of the fire truck as they had ordered. He came into the station afterward and told the Inspector and me all about it. So after they got their money and let him go, they came back to kill him. I suppose they were scared he might be able to say who they were."

This was still a secret, and he asked her to promise she would not tell anyone else about it. He felt that by sharing secrets in this way, it created another kind of bond between them that enriched their relationship.

6   *The Fireman*

As soon as the long interview with the police was finished, Ikuo went straight to the hospital where Michitaro had been admitted. When he got there, he was greeted by a night nurse and a man in a white coat who gave him a hard look and told him that Michitaro was not to have any visitors. It was easy to guess that the man was a detective put there to guard Michitaro.

Ikuo was wondering what he should do next when he saw his old lover, the nurse, coming toward him with her finger on her lips.

"I'll be finished soon and I want to talk to you. Wait for me out in the lobby, will you?"

She spoke to him coolly and hurried away. When he had heard the name of the hospital where Michitaro had been taken, he had half hoped that they might meet again.

She came out to the lobby where he was waiting, wearing a tight blouse that accentuated the size of her breasts. The sight of her awoke pleasurable memories in him.

"I'm thirsty," he said. "I was with the police for ten hours without a break. This is the third day. They keep asking the same thing over and over again."

"They don't have any choice. The victim is still unconscious, and they have no other leads to go on. I suppose you want a beer, so we might as well go over to my place. I've got some in the fridge."

She spoke easily and took his arm. He was not sure how he should take this, but he had to admit that he wanted to go somewhere familiar to rest.

They went to her apartment, and he drank the beer she gave him in one go then glanced over at his ex-lover as she changed out of her clothes. He walked over to the window.

"This apartment is O.K., but I wish you would move somewhere a bit better. It gives me the shivers just to look at an old wooden building like this. It's like living in a pile of firewood."

"Are you still worried about the arsonist? Well, you needn't be. He is unconscious in the intensive care ward at the hospital."

"How do you know about that?" Ikuo asked, raising his voice in surprise.

"I have been interrogated by the police, too, you know. They told me it was my duty as a citizen to help the police, but at the same time, they told me some things they thought I should know about the patient. He is not just the victim of a kidnapping, you know. He is also an arsonist. It was because he set fire to the house where the woman lived with that lion that he was kidnapped."

Ikuo did not say anything but continued to look out the window. There was a car parked on the other side of the

178

road, just beyond the reach of the streetlight, and two men were changing places in it. One of them was clearly Ikuo's old childhood friend, the detective.

"To what extent are you cooperating with the police?" he asked.

"I reply to their questions, but that's about it."

She took some beans out of the freezer and started to cook them, indicating that he should take a shower. He sensed that the chill that had come between them was starting to thaw.

As he was washing himself in the shower, he wondered how the police had found out about Michitaro being the arsonist. At one time he thought this was a secret shared only by him and the kidnappers.

If they know it was Michitaro, why are they still keeping me under surveillance?

He also wondered just how involved the nurse had become in their investigations, but the shower water became too hot and he broke off that chain of thought. More than anything, the thought of his old lover's naked body drove all other thoughts out of his mind, and he became so aroused that he found it difficult to hide the fact from her with the bath towel when he went back into the other room.

"The police said you knew him when you were both in nursery school."

"Yes, I wasn't aware that he was my childhood friend until recently. When we were about five years old, we had been playing with matches and there was a fire. A man died."

"His father, you mean. Is that why you decided to become a fireman?"

She rubbed her cheek against his aroused body as she used to when they were still lovers.

"We have really grown apart, haven't we," she said. "You know, I was sure you were the arsonist."

He felt that something wasn't right, but he could not put his finger on it. He told himself there was no point in worrying about it and reached out to fondle her breast.

"I wish you would tell me about that time. We don't know anything about each other's pasts, do we?"

"That's true."

But he wondered if the day would ever come when they could really understand each other. He tried to remember the day they had first met.

They had been on a crowded train, and she had stomped on his foot so hard that he had almost cried out. She had apologized when they got off, and they had gone for a meal together. The meal led to a movie, then a beer hall, and it had seemed only natural that he come back here to her bed afterward. As far as he could recall, from the very first moment when they had touched on the train, their relationship was based on sex rather than on conversation.

"Who was it who lit the first match?"

"There were three of us, and I can't remember now who had started it. It was when we were children, and twenty-six years have passed since then." He had been asked that same question ever since the fire occurred, and he had always replied that he did not know. But for some reason he found himself saying something that he had never said to another person before. "To be honest, I would like to know the truth about that fire myself."

He sounded so serious that she withdrew her hand in surprise. "What do you mean by that?"

"Well, it's true that we had been playing with matches. We must have lit hundreds of them, but for some reason I get the feeling that an adult lit the fire and then made it look as if it was our fault."

"But why? Do you have any proof?"

"I don't know why. I have no proof. It's just a feeling I get every now and then."

"Maybe you are just trying to escape from a childish sense of guilt."

"That may be true, but there is also my experience as a fireman. We had tired of playing with matches and had gone to play outside before the fire started. I know that one of the matches we had struck could have set something on fire, but we did not start a fire and then run away in fear. This is very important. In the papers at the time, it said that we had watched the fire spread to the paper doors before we ran away but had been scared to admit it afterward. The newspapers were all the same, children playing with fire, tearful mothers, but I cannot help feeling that the truth was different."

"There was also what you saw upstairs . . . the dead man."

"How do you know about that?"

"The police showed me the old newspapers about the case, and I learned all kinds of things about all of you."

Ikuo felt there was something strange about her explanation, but he pushed his suspicions aside.

"I am the only one who saw it. Michitaro wouldn't come upstairs with me."

"What did you see?"

"I had forgotten about it all these years, but now that you ask it comes back to me clearly. Nobody was dead. His father wasn't dead, but he was naked like I am now, lying on his side. There was a woman lying on top of him, and as far as I could make out then, she was tearing the flesh off him, although now that I am an adult, I realize they were making love. He turned and looked at me as I crouched there in terror, then his features suddenly relaxed and he gave a terrible cry as if he had died. I realize now that it had been a cry of ecstasy, but at the time I was so terrified that I flew down the stairs and escaped."

"Did you tell anyone what you had seen?"

"I think I may have told one or two people about it after the fire, but they didn't believe me. I must have made it sound like a fairy tale about demons eating people, and I also told the story about a fire-breathing man. Truth and lies get mixed up in the minds of children until they can't distinguish between them. Also, they said that Michitaro's father was upstairs on his own, and they wouldn't believe a child like me."

"No, someone must have believed you and made sure your I.D. and driver's license would be found in the stomach of the lion. Otherwise it would be too much of a coincidence that all three of you should be caught up in a arson case again after all these years," she said, looking quite pale.

"Who was it then? Who believed the child that was me?"

"I don't know, maybe it was God. I used to go to Sunday school as a child, and I can still remember them telling me that God knows everything we do and that we would learn this when we were older. It made a great impression on me."

She did not say any more. Instead of talking about their childhood, her hot tongue was busy on his erection, and then she drew him into her.

6   *The Arsonist*

Michitaro opened his eyes weakly. For some reason, he knew that death was not far away. Never again would he speed along in his sports car or date girls, and never again would he be able to perform his ritual of fire. It had brought him fulfillment and pleasure, but in the end it had proved to be a curse from which he could not free himself.

He felt that if he was going to die, to close his eyes for the last time, he wanted to confess to someone everything that he had done.

"Are you awake?"

He could see the vague figure of a person and realized that if he was going to speak to someone before he died, then it was going to be to this person.

He reached out to the figure, and it took his hand tenderly. It might be a woman, but as long as it was not his mother, he did not care.

"I lit the fires. Please tell everyone. I am going to die soon, and once I do there will be no more arson attacks."

"Do you really think so? If you die, won't the other person continue to light the fires?"

The misty figure spoke in a gentle whisper, but he found

himself overcome with rage. *Who was this person who spoke as if they knew everything?*

"No, the person you mean, that person doesn't start the fires!" he shouted and suddenly felt weak. His blood pressure was starting to drop.

"You are about to die. There is no reason for you to hide the truth. God knows everything. There is no need for you to hide anything. There is no need for you to try to protect that person."

That voice, that gentle, angel-like voice, could it be the voice of a priest? Although he was not a Catholic himself, he felt that before he died, he would like to be able to confess all his sins to a priest and be absolved of them before he had to meet his Maker.

"I lit the fires," he said in a weak voice.

"We know that, but you only did it to cover up for the fact that the other person had started to light fires, didn't you?"

He tried to deny it; after all, that had been the whole reason for his life, but his head seemed to move against his will, and he nodded in agreement. He found that the act of confession filled him with joy and peace.

"How old were you when you first found out that she was an arsonist?"

"I think it was when I was just finishing junior high school—no, it was after I had entered high school. She was worried about my university entrance exams."

"When did you first realize?"

"She started to go out in the car late at night, and I thought she had a lover. She was everything to me, and the thought that I might lose her to another man was too much to bear. One night when she went out, I followed her on my bike and saw her leave the car, dressed all in black. She disappeared into the night, and a few minutes later flames roared up into the sky.

"I thought she did it to work off her frustrations. But one day, the top student in the class was in the hospital. It was nothing to do with her. He had been involved in a traffic accident, but as a result, I got the highest mark in the class in a test, and that month she didn't set any fires. She knew I was not the cleverest person in the school. In fact, she bought me a motorcycle and told me that I should not bother with school. She said I should become a dropout like my father, but she didn't mean it. I studied harder, and when I received a score within the top five in the class, there were no more fires, but if I dropped below that, she would light one fire a month without fail."

After such a long speech, he became very thirsty, and the shadowy person gave him a drink of water with a practiced hand.

"Why did you always set fire to cardboard boxes?"

"It was not always boxes, it is just that she detested lazy housewives. She thought that being a housewife was a kind of vocation and even gave lectures on the merits of cleaning up one's own mess. It was almost an obsession with her. She hated the arrogance of city people who thought that if they just left their rubbish lying out in the street, someone else would come and clean it up for them. I think that in the beginning her anger and her worry combined and found expression in the fires, but after a while, it became a habit with her, and she just lit them to rid herself of stress.

"Even after I graduated from the university, she still went

out to light fires once every three to six months, and although most of them did not amount to much, just a little smoldering rubbish, one day an old, bedridden man died in a fire that was caused by her. It was when I was thinking of getting married, and I decided then that no matter what I had to do, I must stop her and save her from being branded as an arsonist. In order to achieve this, I went out and lit fires before she had the chance. You must have heard the story about the alcoholic who stopped drinking because his friend always got drunk first and he had to look after him. Well, it's true. I started to light fires of my own and made sure she knew about it, and, would you believe it, no sooner did I start than she stopped. She seemed to be convinced that I had inherited the trait from her, and she really worried about it. I even burned my pet poodle to death as a warning to her, and that gave her a genuine shock. She erected a statue in its memory at the Kaenji Temple."

All the talking had exhausted him, and although it had felt good to get it all off his chest at the beginning, he began to feel that it was futile. Was it really true, what he was saying? What was the truth?

"Is that really the only reason why you killed your pet poodle and went around setting all those fires? You are going to die soon, so why don't you just make a clean breast of it now while you still can?"

The shadowy figure squeezed his hand encouragingly.

Why not . . . why not tell everything I know? Tell them what has been worrying me for so many years?

"That person . . . she . . . my father . . ."

"What did she do?"

"She killed him. That day twenty-six years ago, when

there was the fire, Ikuo went up to the second floor and saw my father killed."

"That's right, she killed your father. You did the right thing. You set those fires in an effort to learn the truth. You did it to scare her into admitting what she had done. You did it to make your mother admit that she had killed your father . . ."

So saying, the shadowy figure walked over and stood beside Michitaro's life-support system. She looked and saw that he had lost consciousness again, and then without any further hesitation, she turned off the machine.

PART SEVEN

1   *The Detective*

Ryosaku stood at the back of the funeral parlor and looked on as he waited for Michitaro's funeral to finish. He saw an old lady in mourning clothes, sitting in a wheelchair, her head held up proudly, but her expression hidden by a pair of dark glasses.

Chieko was pushing the wheelchair, her usual white uniform neglected in favor of a black suit, which was more fitting for the situation. It would appear that the old woman's inheritance was more important to her than his love after all.

In order to get his mind off her, he went over and stood next to the fireman, who was also attending, wearing a mourner's armband.

"Now that he is dead, do you think we have seen the end of the cardboard-box fires?"

Ikuo looked thoughtful before answering.

"I don't know. There will probably be people who want to copy him. Arson is an epidemic crime."

"That's not what I meant. Do you think we've seen the last of these fires that were set in order to lay the blame on you?"

"I don't know. He admitted lighting the fires, but he didn't say anything about trying to lay the blame on me. I made that point when I was being interrogated, and for the sake of his honor, I would like to stress it again."

"Do you mean there was someone else who fed your documents to the lion?"

"Well, I'm pretty sure it was not him. I think it would have been impossible."

"I agree with you there, but do you think he knew about it when he lit the fire?"

"No, I don't. When I spoke to him, he seemed eager to tell me everything."

"What did he think about your documents being found like that?"

"I don't know, but I expect he just thought it was co-incidence like everyone else. Then again, he might have thought that the lion's owner fed them to the lion herself in order to get back at me. Either way, he seemed to consider it an act of Divine Providence that it resulted in my getting the blame for the fire. He appeared to be a great believer in the workings of fate."

"Divine Providence," Ryosaku repeated thoughtfully, "that's a good expression. By the way, did I mention that the kidnappers sent us a copy of the tape containing his confession?"

"Why do you think they did that? Is it some kind of challenge?"

"Well, I suppose there is that, too, but I think they want to show that they had kept their promise and released him. They say they only kidnapped him in an effort to find out the truth behind the fire and that it was not they who ran him over after he was released."

"Did they send a copy of the tape to the press?" asked Ikuo.

"No, apparently as a condition for getting the money, they agreed not to publish anything that would discredit him. They are just very angry about being blamed for his death."

"But if they are innocent, who do you think it was who killed him?"

Ikuo looked puzzled. He had assumed that the kidnappers had gone back on their word and killed him.

"Maybe it was just a coincidence and he was run over by a drunk. It could have been the work of Providence."

"You may be right. It could easily have been Providence. If he had lived, he would have been sent to prison and made to spend the greater part of his life away from other people. But what meaning was there to his life? What did he achieve between the time we played together as children and now?"

Ryosaku shook his head. "Who can tell. But to get back to the present, you are still not free of suspicion, you know. There is still the case of the TV actress. I am not saying that you killed her and tried to set her apartment on fire, but you went to her room and slept with her that day, didn't you?"

Ikuo remained silent, but Ryosaku took that to be an admission, and his voice became softer.

"The identification division says it can definitely prove that those jogging shoes were yours. They were purchased from the fire brigade's shop and given as a prize at the sports day last autumn.   ey were very good quality shoes and had a maker's number inside them. What made you leave them behind? You don't have to say anything that will incriminate you. We will take a statement later."

"The dog chewed them up, and the girl loaned me a pair of sandals to wear home. Of course, she was still as fit as ever and could talk when I left."

"You should have come to the police as soon as you heard about the case and given a statement."

"I did not want to be arrested."

"The police are not all fools, you know."

Even as Ryosaku said this, he realized that deep inside he suspected Ikuo, and even if Ikuo were found to be one hundred percent innocent, he would still suspect him.

"If someone is really trying to make you take the blame for all these fires, I don't think we have heard the last of it. Apparently your blood type is O. They found semen in the dead actress's body that was type O, but I hope we won't find that nurse over there dead in a fire with type-O semen inside her."

He nodded toward Chieko, who was pushing the old woman's wheelchair away from the funeral parlor toward a large limousine. Ikuo did not change his expression.

"I am type A and Michitaro was AB. If we are to believe that this is all the work of fate, then surely there should be someone with B type. Maybe that person is the real murderer." Then, without looking at the detective, Ikuo added, "She is B type."

192

"You mean the nurse? Don't be ridiculous. Do you have some reason to be suspicious of her?"

"The night the woman with the lion died, I went out on my patrol from her room."

"Leaving her filled with O-type semen, I presume."

Even as Ryosaku spoke, he wondered what was wrong with him. He had no right to feel jealous of the fireman. After all, Chieko had been his lover then.

"Ever since the night of the fire, I have thought about my documents. Quite some time later, I realized that I had not dropped them in the garden of the woman with the lion. I am quite sure I left them on the chest of drawers in her room."

Ryosaku thought over what this would mean, and then he tried to visualize just where in the girl's room Ikuo meant.

"Are you trying to say that after you left, she took your documents and delivered them to someone who fed them to the lion?"

"Yes, but the only problem is that as soon as I left, she took some sleeping pills and fell into a deep sleep. Taking sleeping pills is one of her bad habits, you know."

"Well, you must have taken the documents with you then. You had quite an argument with the woman with the lion. She could easily have taken your wallet from your back pocket and fed it to her lion in a fit of temper. You should not think about it too much. You'll drive yourself crazy."

"I already have," Ikuo said with a shrug.

"Anyway, that girl is not like that. I have known her for a long time, you know. She looked after my wife when she was in the hospital. She is not like us. She doesn't do her job because she has to. She really enjoys it."

He spoke brightly and slapped Ikuo on the back in a friendly way, telling himself that he had absolutely no reason to suspect her.

2   The Fireman

Michitaro's mother led Ikuo down to the workshop under the garage. The flower beds around the basement were lower than the rest of the garden, allowing natural light into the room, and it did not have the damp feel that is usually associated with basements. When he thought about the various preparations that Michitaro had made here before going out to light the fires, he felt he could understand the other's loneliness a little better.

"I would like to return the lighter, matches, and bag of gasoline that you gave me on my last visit. I thought about it, and I decided not to put them into the bag with the money after all."

"Why not? That was what he wanted, wasn't it?"

She picked up the lighter and looked at it with deep emotion.

"Because it occurred to me that they were fakes. What he really wanted were . . ." He broke off for a moment, then making up his mind, he continued. "I realized that what he really wanted were the lighter and bag of gasoline that you used and the actual matches that you rescued from the fire twenty-six years ago."

"I am afraid I don't understand a word of what you're saying."

She held her hands in front of her like a little girl, and

he felt he could see the trace of a smile in the depths of her eyes.

"He copied your method of arson. His motive in lighting the fires was to act as a warning to you, or rather, he thought that if he lit the fires first, you would stop. If he was lighting the fires for his own sake, he would not use such an old-fashioned method. He could quite easily make a remote-control device or a timer."

"Why do you have to make up these aspersions about me? I have lost both my husband and my son due to fires."

"I'm not making it up. I'm only passing on what Michitaro told me." He was bluffing, but he knew in his bones that he was right, and he felt that he owed it to his old childhood friend to find out the truth if he could.

"He always did have a good imagination. I thought we knew each other so well, but it would appear that he misunderstood me."

"That may be true for the recent fires, but when he was five, he didn't need to understand anything. He knew what he saw."

"And what, may I ask, was that?"

"He saw you pour gasoline on the dead man upstairs and set fire to him."

Hearing his words, she clutched her chest as if she were in pain and started to laugh uncontrollably.

"Don't be ridiculous. You're making it all up. You have no proof, but you still try to discredit me. You shouldn't go around slandering people like that, you know."

"Even at the time, some people thought you had killed your husband, but there was no evidence, so they could not do anything. Now it is different. The little seeds of proof that had lain around all these years have finally sprung into bloom. The proof is in the memories of five-year-old boys, memories coupled with an adult's judgment. Now we know exactly what happened twenty-six years ago."

"That is not proof. It is no more than groundless and malicious rumor."

She started to laugh in the same affected way, but her voice failed her, and a look of pain came over her features.

"When you ran into the fire to gather up the burned matches we had dropped there, you acted the part of a loving mother whose only concern was to hide all the evidence of your son's guilt. That was the way people looked at it at the time, but really there was another explanation."

He paused and took a deep breath. He almost wished that he smoked, as the action of lighting a cigarette would give him time to collect his thoughts. She seemed to sense his thoughts and took out a long, thin, filter-tipped cigarette, which she lit with a gold lighter.

"The real reason why you frantically collected all the children's dead matches was to leave everyone else with the impression that the real culprits responsible for the fire were the children. That was the reason why you continued to persecute the children afterward in front of other adults, and so successful were you that the family of one of the children found themselves unable to live in this area any longer."

She still did not say anything in her defense but just stood there, watching the smoke rise from her cigarette.

"Another thing I can understand better now is the dog that was found to have died with your husband. You claimed that you had just stepped out to pick it up when the fire started, but that was not true. It was a vital part of your plan. You had taken it to the vet's the day before, knowing that when you brought it back, it would rush up to see your husband the minute it came in through the door. When you came home, you went upstairs and poured gasoline around the room before going back down to collect all the matches we had dropped. When you had done that, you let the terrier out of its cage and did something unforgivable. You soaked his tail in gasoline, set fire to it, and let him run up to your husband."

As he spoke, he could see the past unfold before his eyes like a movie.

"Why are you confident about all these things when you could never have seen them yourself? Why do you try to slander me like this? It is not just me. Why do you want to slander my husband and son? What have you against us?"

"That's where you're wrong. Your son and I saw it all. You may not have realized it, or maybe you did but ignored us. Either way, Michitaro and I had returned to the house, but as we did so we heard you come in and we were scared you would tell us off, so we hid under the sofa. An adult would never think of looking there, but for us, it was one of many hiding places in our secret jungle.

"When you came in, you first went upstairs, then you came back down to the entrance hall. When we heard the dog whining, we crawled out to see what had happened and were just in time to see it rush up the stairs with its tail on fire. After that we were terrified and ran away again."

"You're lying. Don't think that you can threaten me with stories like that. You weren't even there. You were all playing in the park a long way away. That fire started in a cupboard downstairs. One of the matches you had been playing with had set fire to some old cotton mattresses, and the smoke had risen up to my husband's room directly above. There had been a bottle of benzene by his bed, that is true, but that was to clean off the blood that he coughed up. The police and the fire brigade were quite satisfied with the cause of the fire. It was just unfortunate that my husband had been asleep at the time. He suffered from tuberculosis and he had caught a cold so he had taken some sleeping pills and didn't awaken in time. That's why you were forbidden from going upstairs to play."

She stared at him sadly.

"That is a lie. That day you were naked in bed with him, having sex. I saw you."

"Will you stop it! I have had enough of your lewd lies and innuendoes! I will not have any more of it. I have not done anything that I should feel ashamed of, and if you really must know, my husband had not shared my bed for six months prior to the fire."

She glared angrily at him, and he could not think of anything more to say.

3   *The Arsonist*

Michitaro's mother walked through the main gate of the Kaenji Temple and over to the statue of the poodle standing in the corner of the temple grounds.

She had brought the lighter, burned matches, and the bag of gasoline with her, and she thought how fitting it would be if she were to have them buried at the foot of the statue. But that was not to be. She had no way of knowing that they would not be discovered someday. She realized that it would be much safer if she was to have them burned and destroyed forever.

She stood in front of the statue of the poodle that was, for her, symbolic of her son. She wanted to kneel before it and plant a kiss on its cold surface, but something stopped her. Instead she turned and walked toward the temple.

"That policeman was here asking all kinds of questions, but I just said I did not know anything, and I think that I managed to get rid of him. You want me to burn these things, too, do you? I will purify the ashes and sprinkle them in front of the statue of the dog." The young priest took the bag of things from her reverently.

"I have spoken to the chief priest," she said, "and he agrees that the best thing would be to purify the things by burning them. You don't have to worry about the police." She spoke in a firm voice, and then, giving him a large donation for the temple, she made her way to the priests' quarters.

What could the police be investigating? She had already lost her husband and her son. What more could they want?

"Those things I brought today and the things I brought before are all the things that my son used when he lit those fires. I would be most grateful if you could burn them all and sprinkle the ashes in the temple grounds," she said, bowing deeply to the chief priest. Now that her son was dead, this temple was all she had, and it was only natural that she should donate all the insurance money received from his death to the temple. They were sure to think that she was just acting as a bereaved mother ought to act. They would never guess that she was using them to hide the evidence of a crime. Only a low-minded person would think that.

"That young detective is very persistent," the priest said, looking at her with gentle eyes. He had the peaceful look peculiar to priests, and he seemed incapable of doubt.

"Yes, he was an old friend of my son. He was one of the children who were playing with matches when our house caught fire, and I suppose he never managed to get over it. I know that my son didn't either and that it was the fire that was responsible for him becoming an arsonist."

"I see. He has my sympathy, but it explains why he was so interested about what happened twenty-six years ago. He said there had been another statue of a dog set up in this temple soon after that fire and asked me to look into it. Well, I became interested. His enthusiasm is quite infectious, and I went through the old records from that period. He was right, you know. Three months after the fire at your house, a statue of a guardian dog was donated to the temple and there was a note saying it was in memory of a terrier that died in a fire. The date the terrier is said to have died is the same as the fire at your house, and you did lose a terrier in the fire, didn't you?"

"Yes, its body was found next to my husband's. It was as if it had tried to protect him from the fire."

"There is one other thing, however. It occurred to me that whoever it was that dedicated the statue may also have copied some sutras at the same time, so I decided to take a look. The sutras are dedicated to the lord Buddha, and I am not really permitted to look at them, but I thought it might have some connection to the tragedy you have experienced, so I took it upon myself to go through them, and what do you think I found? On the same day that the statue was dedicated, someone had written a sutra in your husband's name, and in the space left for wishes, was written, 'That the perpetrator die by fire.' Your husband was already dead at that time so he could not have written the sutra himself, and I realized that, as you were the one who had borne the brunt of the sorrow, you had probably written it for him.

"Buddha teaches forgiveness, and your son is already dead. Don't you think it would be best if you were to take back your request before anything happens to the other two people who had been playing with your son when the fire started?" He spoke these last words rather forcefully.

"Have you mentioned this to anyone else?" she asked, without changing her expression.

"Of course not. I would never speak of anything so private to anyone but the person who wrote it. You have dedicated two dogs to this temple. The first was in the time of my predecessor's predecessor, so I cannot comment about that, but now that your son has died, I feel you should take back your request."

"You are very kind. Will you return the sutra to me?"

She took the yellowed paper from the priest, and, after telling him about the insurance money she wanted to donate to the temple, she went outside. She sat on a seat under a maple tree and read the sutra to herself.

Who could have written it? Who could have asked for such a terrible thing, and in her husband's name? What did it mean?

Obviously it had been written in the hope that whoever started that fire should be punished by fire. She noticed that her hand, which was holding the paper, was trembling slightly. She had lost her husband twenty-six years ago, and now she had lost her only son, but she had never allowed herself to give in. Why should she be scared now? If she was going to be punished, it would have happened a long time ago. Most important, the law was helpless to punish her now. The statute of limitations had expired, and she could never be held responsible for the death of her husband and the burning of her house. Who could punish her now for something she had done when she was still young, twenty-six years ago? She crushed the old sutra in her hand.

"This is lucky. When I inquired at the temple, they said I would find you over here."

She looked up and saw the young detective. He had his jacket over his arm and was panting slightly. She hurriedly hid the crushed-up sutra behind her bag.

"I know I have already asked you about it, but are you sure you didn't dedicate a statue of a dog to this temple before? It was a long time ago, twenty-six years ago, after the fire at your house."

"The priest asked me about it, too, but I can only repeat that I know absolutely nothing about any such statue. I don't even remember having seen such a statue, so why are you so persistent in asking me?"

"I see. It is just that I remember seeing it here. These days I have been thinking about it a lot, and I can remember quite distinctly being dragged here and questioned about the fire. It was true that we had been playing with matches, but I would not admit it. I cried and looked around, and there, close by, was the brand-new statue of a dog. It had a fierce face and glaring eyes, and I remember I was so scared of it that I almost wet myself. I was told that if I did not own up to having lit the fire, I would be buried under the statues."

"Who told you?"

"You did, I think," he said in embarrassment.

She remembered that he had been the strongest-willed of the three children, and he had acted as if he never did anything wrong.

"I have forgotten everything about that period in my life, and I have no desire to remember. I do seem to recall, though, that when the fire started you three children were playing in a park some distance away, or had Ikuo and Michitaro come back to the house?"

"I am afraid I cannot remember clearly. Now that you ask, I do seem to recall that we were playing hide-and-seek. I was 'it,' and the other two had gone back to the house to hide. Then again, I also seem to remember that we were playing on the slide in the park. I cannot be sure." He shook his head.

So Ikuo lied. They didn't see anything. The thought that her son might have seen her was more than she could bear.

"Did Michitaro ever come here to copy the sutras?" Ryosaku asked.

"No, he wasn't interested in that sort of thing."

"Yes, I can imagine. Two days after the fire, someone wrote a sutra and signed it with Ikuo Onda's name, but when I asked him about it, he said that it was not him. I asked at the temple, and they said it was written by a young man who looked like a student. It is strange, isn't it?"

He shook his head in bewilderment. The police were checking out all sorts of leads, but they did not seem to be getting anywhere. At least, it did not seem as if Michitaro's mother was connected with the case at all.

4 *The Detective*

Ryosaku stood at attention in front of the Chief Inspector's desk. The Chief Inspector stood looking out of the window, his hands clasped behind his back.

"You can stop your investigation of the fireman," he said without turning.

"But why, sir? There is still the chance he was involved in the murder of that actress," Ryosaku said nervously, not sure how the Inspector would react.

"We have caught the fire breather. He got into a fight in a brothel outside the city, and when he was arrested he admitted to committing arson in Tokyo. He is an Algerian with a French passport, and he used to work as a fire eater in the same circus as the woman with the lion. He was always getting drunk and starting fights over women, so he was given the sack after a year and worked as a street performer after that. He was brought to Japan to perform at the opening of a department store, and he stayed on here afterward. He met the woman with the lion when he was working for the department store, and she asked him to set her house on fire so she could claim the insurance money on her lion. He lit the fire by blowing burning alcohol out of his mouth. He wore a leather gypsy outfit when he performed and that was what the woman next door had seen when she said she had seen a fire-breathing, batlike man outside the house."

"But what about Michitaro? We have a tape recording of him admitting to the fire, and, anyway, the gang had only kidnapped him because they thought he was the arsonist."

"Yes, but it may have been the gang that got him to admit to starting the fire in order to cover up for themselves. You must remember, the kidnapping was never made public, and there is no proof to back up Michitaro's confession. Although those fires all appear to have been connected, they could just as easily have been a coincidence.

"When I first joined the force, there was a fire at a summer house in Karuizawa where seven people died. Among the dead there was a famous politician whom I was assigned to guard and a popular hostess who owned a bar in Ginza. The bodies were covered with terrible wounds, and I was convinced they had been murdered and then the house burned to hide the evidence. I worked all out on the case, but it was discovered that the fire was caused by a gas leak in the bathroom, and the wounds on the bodies were made by falling debris when the house collapsed. After that I tended to look at cases from a simpler point of view, and, you know, the majority of them are merely a series of coincidences."

He turned and looked directly at Ryosaku.

"When this series of fires started, especially after the one in which the lion died, I felt that for the first time I was being confronted with crime on a grand scale and that this time there was more to it than mere coincidence. I thought the curtain was rising on a splendid crime with a carefully planned plot and actors that had spent years in preparation of their parts, but I was wrong. With the arrest of this fire breather, the whole thing has become very pedestrian. Even if you continue to trail that fireman, nothing is going to happen. The drama I thought we were going to be treated to never existed, and there was probably not even an audience to watch it."

Ryosaku felt like a child who has had his favorite toy taken away, and he pouted.

"I'm afraid I cannot understand a word of what you say, sir."

"Well, let me explain. Twenty-six years ago, when you were still in nursery school, there was a fire at the home of an up-and-coming young painter. As the chief of the local police station, the case was put in my charge. I was still very young. I couldn't have been much older than you are now, and it left a big impression on me."

He turned back to the window and looked out thoughtfully. He had received a law degree from the university, and when he joined the police force, he must have been considered one of the elite to have been put in charge of a police station at such a young age.

Confronted by this sudden confession, Ryosaku did not know what to say for a few moments.

"So you knew about Ikuo and me, and that was why you ordered me to devote myself to the inquiry, is it?"

"Yes, like you, that case affected my whole life. You three were formidable opponents. I stayed up late every night studying books on child psychology in an effort to get the truth out of you, but it was no good. You were the most stubborn of the lot. You insisted that you had been playing on the swings and slides in the park all day and that you had not been playing with matches at all."

Hearing this, Ryosaku blushed.

"What about the other two?"

"Ikuo was very cautious. He didn't deny anything and he wouldn't admit anything either, but I got the feeling that he was hiding something. Michitaro would just burst into tears when I tried to ask him anything, and there was nothing I could do. All of you resisted to the end and tried to protect yourselves from us grown-ups."

Ryosaku thought it was rather unfair that his superior should have kept all this from him until now and felt a little angry, but that was because he was embarrassed to hear about the lies he had told as a child.

"When I first heard that Ikuo's I.D. had been found in the stomach of the lion, I felt that it was connected somehow. I felt that some huge drama was about to unfold, although, of course, I had my reasons for thinking so. Michitaro had come to me before and told me about his mother's tendencies toward arson."

"You mean that you were aware of such an important fact?" Ryosaku asked, looking even more unsatisfied.

"Yes, I once considered becoming Michitaro's stepfather, you know," he said, keeping his face turned to the window as he admitted his love for Michitaro's mother.

"Twenty-six years ago, Yoriko was suspected of having killed her husband. We had anonymous letters stating this, and society as a whole seemed to suspect her. We made our inquiries along those lines, but it turned out that she was innocent. There had been an adult witness at the scene of the crime, but we kept the fact secret to protect her privacy.

She was a twenty-one-year-old trainee nurse from the local hospital who was having an affair with Michitaro's father. She used to visit on the pretense of delivering medicine for him, and they enjoyed sex together when his wife was out of the house. She was upstairs until shortly before the fire broke out, and she said that she could hear you children playing downstairs and that shortly before she left she had smelled something burning. At that time Michitaro's mother was still at the vet's picking up the terrier, so she had a firm alibi and it was a simple open-and-shut case, superficially at any rate."

The Inspector turned back toward him, and he tried to visualize the older man when he had been young and in love. The Inspector had been put in charge of an investigation, but he had fallen in love with one of the main suspects. Ryosaku could not help but draw parallels with his own affair with Chieko. The Inspector had been lucky enough to get through it without destroying his career, and now he could stand there and talk fondly of it as if it had happened to another man.

"But if that fire eater is not the real arsonist, he may change his testimony in court," stated Ryosaku.

"If he is being used as a scapegoat, you can be sure that a suitable sum of money has been sent to his family. People like him are very attached to their families, and there is not much they will not do if it means they can send some money back to them from overseas. This is just a simple case of arson. At any rate, there are certain people with money who want us to think so, and if that is the case, there is nothing we can do to prove otherwise."

"So you mean this gypsy used to walk around at night

setting people's houses on fire whenever he was drunk, and that he lit the fire in which the lion died as a favor to an old friend in order to defraud the insurance company?"

"If that's what he says, why not? The important thing is that there will be no more fires."

"But what about the murder of that actress? We have the evidence of the jogging shoes, so why don't we arrest him?"

"There is no need to go that far. Everything will sort itself out if we just leave it."

The Inspector did not sound very convinced himself, and Ryosaku wondered if he was calling off the investigation for the sake of his old lover or whether it was because he was being pressured by the people with money that he had mentioned. It was not for him to suspect a man who was about to retire, so he just saluted and marched crisply out of the room.

As he walked down the corridor, he could not help but think it a shame that the Chief Inspector had chosen to blot his copybook and act in such an unprofessional way just before he left the force.

5   *The Fireman*

Ikuo was awakened from a deep sleep by a call from the nurse. Her voice was low and hesitant.

"It said on the television that a fire eater has admitted to setting the fire that killed the woman with the lion, but that's not true. It was Michitaro who started the fire, you know that. . . ."

"I don't care who started that fire, I've lost interest in that case," Ikuo said irritably.

"But you mustn't. This involves you. I think you will be cross when you hear what I have to say, but I will say it anyway. I will probably be killed myself soon. Someone will come and pour gasoline over me and set a light to it. I have known that it would happen for a long time."

"Don't be ridiculous. If you think like that, you will go mad."

"You only say that because you don't know anything. Oh well, I may as well tell you, while I still have the time. Michitaro set fire to that house with the lion in order to make you take the blame. Someone asked me, I can't tell you who it was, but they asked me to give them your license and I.D. You had often forgotten them after you had slept with me and went out on your silly patrols. This person knew all about your patrols. They knew everything about you. They knew that you were a methodical man and that you would not hesitate to impose your views on others if you thought you were in the right, and they even knew about your playing with matches twenty-six years ago. I know you will probably be disappointed to hear this, but I trod on your foot in the train that time because that person asked me to. The reason I smiled at you when we met on the platform, the reason I went to the restaurant with you and then to the beer hall and finally to my apartment to stay the night was all because that person paid me to do what they asked. Yes, that one wanted you to come to my apartment so you would start your patrols in this area, and sure enough, when the fires started, your sense of justice and your habit of poking your nose into things made you go out on your midnight patrols. The whole thing was to make you start your patrols, and although I thought that it had to be a joke, I did what I was told, and, sure enough, you acted just as they had predicted. No, don't hang up. I want to admit everything to you. Then I can die in peace."

Listening to Chieko's sad voice on the phone, he shook with anger, which quickly changed to despair. At least he now knew that he had been right about his I.D., but he was amazed to hear that the look of terrible embarrassment she had given him when she trod on his foot in the train had been just an act.

"You remember I told you that when you went out I could not sleep and took sleeping pills regularly? Well, that was a lie, too. I only said it to fool you. Actually I went out to see that person as soon as you left."

"What would you have done if I had stopped going out on patrol, in order to make you stop taking the pills?"

"I don't know. In that case, I might have really started to love you, but as it was, you preferred to go out and be a busybody, saying it was for the best."

"I won't argue with you about that now, but it still doesn't excuse you for what you did. You deceived me, and you did it for money. Who was it who asked you to do it? What does he have against me?"

"Michitaro's mother. She was prepared to sacrifice you in order to save her son. She was willing to use all the money that her husband had left her if it meant that she could stop people from knowing that he was the arsonist."

"But why did she choose me to take the blame?"

"Because of what you said twenty-six years ago. You had cried and said that you saw her kill her husband."

"But I was only five years old then."

"Yes, she waited twenty-six years to get her revenge."

"She must be insane."

A fit of rage came upon him, and he wanted to slam the phone down. It was ridiculous to punish someone for something they had done as a child.

"Was it she who tried to make me take the blame for the death of that actress, too?"

"But you slept with her, didn't you? For someone who goes around thinking he is the defender of the weak, you did not seem to hesitate before you slept with a poor girl who had nowhere else to turn."

"She seduced me."

"Well, that's neither here nor there. The problem we are discussing is that fire twenty-six years ago. Did you really see Michitaro's mother kill his father? You told everyone that you did."

"No, I didn't. What I did see was a naked girl sucking off Michitaro's father. Now that I am an adult, I understand they were making love—I have told you this before. What I don't know is whether it was Michitaro's mother or not."

"That naked woman was my mother. When you saw her twenty-six years ago, I still didn't exist. It must have been on that day that I was created. When I first heard our difference in age, it occurred to me that you were witness to my creation.

"You said that I tricked you for money, but that was only half of it. I thought that by bringing that fire back into the public eye, I would be able to show everyone who I was. It gave meaning to my life. I have money, but I have to live in this dirty little apartment, and I had to trick you like that. You can't understand what life is like for me. I was born in Japan and I can only speak Japanese, but due to my nationality I am treated like a second-class person. It was even worse for my mother. Just because she was a Korean, she was persecuted by my father's family. She lost her job and her chances of marriage, and in the end she committed suicide."

"Then why are you working for your father's family now?"

"I can't speak anymore. I'm too exhausted. . . . I just called to say good-bye. . . . Good-bye, my fireman, I really loved you. It was only an act in the beginning, but I loved you in the end. This time I have really taken some sleeping pills, lots of them. . . . What's that noise? He has come. I can smell gasoline . . ."

Her final words were very slurred.

Ikuo jumped up and ran out of the house. He managed to stop a taxi and had it drive toward her apartment as fast as possible. He was filled with love for her.

He would call an ambulance and have them pump out her stomach at the hospital, after which he would propose. He would forget their past and live only for the future. They would have a happy household with lots of children.

All that talk about her being killed was just nonsense. Nobody would want to burn her to death, but why did she say that she could smell gasoline?

Several fire engines roared past his taxi. They would not be able to get to her apartment. The road was too narrow! Her building was surrounded by other old wooden buildings, and the fire would not take long to spread.

God! Please let her be all right!

He jumped out of the taxi and ran toward the fire. There

213

was already quite a crowd of onlookers gathered, but he barged through them and headed for the door of the building. One of his acquaintances from training school grabbed him by the shoulder.

"Let me go through! My fiancée is in there!"

He tore off the other man's helmet and fireproof coat, then, getting one of the men to spray him with a hose, he rushed up the stairs and crawled along the floor. Her room was already ablaze, although the bed had still not caught fire. He felt around on it, but he could not find her.

He expected any moment to hear her voice, but the room was silent. His breath became labored, and he realized that he could not stay there any longer, but still he reached out with both hands, searching for the sweet body of his lover.

Even as his lungs filled with carbon monoxide, he believed her and did not doubt a word she had said.

6   *The Arsonist*

Michitaro's mother put on the glasses that she would never allow herself to be seen wearing in public as she studied the report of Ikuo's death. With Ikuo gone, it meant that two of the three children were now dead. Never for a moment had she ever imagined that they would go before her.

She thought about Ikuo. He had been a strange child, and twenty-six years ago he had said something that almost made people suspect her of killing her husband. She had been doing so well until he started saying those things, but she thought she had managed to put off everyone's suspicions. It had cost her dearly, though. She had had to change the whole course of her life, but now as she looked back on it, it seemed worthwhile.

She walked over to the window and watched the plane trees blowing wildly in the wind.

It said in the papers that he had gone to his girl's apartment, and, after strangling her, he had poured gasoline around the room and set fire to it. It sounded very out of character for him to do something like that, but if he was to be accused of being the arsonist, it meant that she would be quite safe. When he had come around to see her that last time, he had said all kinds of nasty things to threaten her, and it served him right if he was accused of being the arsonist.

Nobody was left who would be able to accuse her of having started that fire twenty-six years ago. There was no proof, but she realized she had been lucky. If she was to do the same thing now, she would probably be caught.

She had held the pillow over his face for five minutes before she poured the gasoline around his bed. She had been sure that she had suffocated him, but there had been evidence of smoke in his lungs, and that was why it was put down as death by fire. Had it really been a crime of passion? No, she had decided some time before that she did not want to remain tied down to a sick man forever, and, even if he had not started that sordid little affair with the nurse, she was no longer faithful to him anyway. She stood at the window shaking her head as she thought over what she had done so long ago.

She had first thought of killing him when the children began to play with matches in the house. She had warned them about it repeatedly, but then one day the idea had come to her. It was as if the devil were tempting her, and no matter how many times she put the idea out of her mind, it kept coming back.

If she put the blame on the children, she could kill her husband and set fire to the house without being caught. She wondered now how things could have seemed so simple to her in those days. Now she would be too scared to act; it was because she was young that she had managed it. The future had seemed so bleak that she had felt it was worth any risk to escape, to punch a hole in the darkness that tried to envelop her.

She knew that her husband had taken out a huge insurance policy in Michitaro's name. He had been a careful man and had worried about what would happen to his son if he were to die. Even though he was a sick man, he used his influence at his father's company to take out a policy. The executives at the company had done him proud, but it was not just the money that drove her to kill him. More than anything, she was worried about what he would do if he found out that Michitaro was not his real son.

When Michitaro had injured himself at nursery school, she had been shocked to learn that his blood type was different from her husband's. When she thought about her lifestyle in Paris before she met her husband, she realized that he could have been anybody's child, but why was it that when he was born, the hospital had said his blood type was the same as her husband's?

She learned later from the police that blood tests could not be one hundred percent accurate. All the same, it had been a cruel trick of fate, and it had led her to commit murder.

She had tied a fuse to his dog's tail and let it run up the stairs, but when she thought of it now, she realized she must have been mad to think that such a harebrained scheme would work. Maybe she had not really wanted to kill her husband, and she only treated his pet like that because she was jealous of the attention it received.

It was all that person's fault. They had tried to break up their marriage from the beginning, and it was they who had first sent that nurse over to look after him. When she had first realized that he was having an affair, she had feigned indifference and spurned him, but really she had been mad with jealousy. She had still been young.

But it had all been for nothing in the end. Michitaro had been her one reason for living, but he was dead now and Ikuo had also died. She no longer felt the energy to compete with that person. Everything seemed pointless, and nothing remained to afford her any pleasure. She guessed that this must be one of the effects of menopause.

But why had Ikuo behaved like he had, and why had he made it appear that he had been the arsonist? It did not seem like him. He had been such a bright child and had never taken any chances.

Her thoughts were interrupted by the buzzing of the front door, and, looking down, she saw that it was the detective. Of the three children, he was the only one left now.

He had always been different from the other two. He had never been afraid of her. All three had sensed what she had done, but he had not been worried by the thought of her crime. All he had worried about had been the punishment he might receive from an adult.

She led him into the living room.

"As I am sure you must have read in the papers, Ikuo betrayed our trust in him. He was the arsonist all along, and now that he is dead the investigation has been brought to a close, and I have come to report to you."

He spoke in a vigorous tone, which she found very pleasant, but it made her feel even more strongly the deaths of Ikuo and her son.

"That nurse was lucky to escape," she commented.

"Yes, she fell unconscious when he strangled her, and she came to when she smelled the gasoline. She got out without much injury, just a burn on the leg, but as you say, she was lucky to escape. Without her testimony we would never have known that Ikuo was the arsonist. We would still be wasting our time looking for someone else. I won't have to visit Kaenji Temple anymore. I felt strangely drawn there while he was still alive."

He smiled brightly.

The minute she heard the nurse's story, she recognized a kindred spirit. She had been lucky. It was because she was young and she had only tried it once that she had got away with it so easily. If she tried it again, she would be caught.

"But why do you think Ikuo decided to go back to the scene of the crime like that? Especially when the fire was burning so fiercely?"

"There are any number of theories. Maybe he remembered some vital piece of evidence that he had left on the scene, or perhaps he wanted to carry out the body of his victim to make it look as if he was a hero. We have no way of knowing for sure, though. Dead men don't tell tales."

218

That is true, she thought. *Twenty-six years ago the papers had claimed all kinds of things, but it was only speculation. As long as the person involved did not say anything, the truth would never come out.*

"You are right," she said aloud, "it's only speculation. Let me show you something. I didn't intend to let anyone else see it, but I'll make an exception for you."

She took out the copy of the sutra the priest had given her and showed it to him.

"What do you make of this?"

" 'That the perpetrator die by fire,' " he said, reading it out loud. "I wonder what it means and who could have written it?"

"I don't know, but I suppose it must be someone who hated the arsonist very much. I wonder what they think now that Ikuo is dead."

"Well, they have no right to feel happy. As far as that fire twenty-six years ago is concerned, Ikuo was blameless. Even when we were children, Ikuo used to walk around with a water pistol and put out the matches as we lit them. I now know exactly what happened that day. After he died, I could not sleep. I stayed up all night thinking about that day, and then suddenly it all came back to me. I started that fire. We had been playing hide-and-seek, and I hid in a cupboard on the first floor. It was filled with cotton that was to be used to make new bed quilts. It was white and fluffy, and it felt like being in a cave in the snow."

"What, like the match girl in the story?"

"No, I wasn't interested in that kind of game. That was Michitaro and Ikuo. I just enjoyed watching things burn. I had a box of matches with me, and I struck them all and watched as the cotton started to smolder. Then I went out and forgot all about it."

"Why didn't you tell anyone afterward?"

"Because even though I was still a child, I realized what a terrible thing I had done and I was scared. I knew I would have to tell someone eventually, but there was nobody for me to talk to. I didn't have a mother to confide in, and as time passed it became even harder to say anything. Now it is different. Michitaro and Ikuo became arsonists because of a fire they had nothing to do with. But not me. I have my own life."

Michitaro's mother had recovered her composure and spoke in her usual tone. "Yes, children don't have any responsibility for what they do. It is the people who made them think they were at fault that should be blamed. It is their education that was at fault."

That's right, I am the one who is to blame for their death, she thought. *If I had not tried to protect myself by insisting for all these years that they were responsible for the fire, those two young men would still be alive today.* After she had seen the detective out, she sat by herself at the dining table and started to laugh hysterically.

When she thought about it, she remembered that she had come back to the house that day and had noticed the smell of smoke, but she never for a minute suspected that the children had really started a fire. She had scolded them repeatedly about playing with matches and had even thought of setting the house on fire and putting the blame on them, but she had not thought that it could actually happen.

To think that when she had held the pillow over her husband's face, sprinkled benzene around his bed, and tied a fuse to the dog's tail, he had already been dead. It had not been Ikuo or Michitaro. It had been the third boy. He had lit a fire in the cupboard directly under the room where her husband had been sleeping, causing him to die of carbon monoxide poisoning. There was no need for her to have spent the last twenty-six years feeling threatened by her crime. She could have lived a fuller life.

She could not believe the pointlessness of it all and sat with her head buried in her hands, laughing and crying for what seemed like an eternity.

PART
EIGHT

1 *The Murderer*

A black shadow slipped silently into Michitaro's house and up to his mother's bedroom. He was wearing black fatigues and a black woolen hat, his face hidden by the collar of his jacket.

He had been trained as a commando, and he had seen plenty of action in Europe and in the Middle East. Now, however, he was not acting on behalf of his country. He was motivated by money, and he felt absolutely no compunction about what he was about to do here in this Far Eastern city. He had already successfully started several fires as he had been ordered to, and he had made them all look as if they were the work of an amateur. The one condition that his employer had made was that he would not be seen by anyone, but that was no problem for him. He did not care if what he did was done for political or personal reasons. As long as his employer paid him what he asked, he would do it, no questions asked. A colleague of his had told him that a group of Japanese in the same profession had been employed to kidnap someone, but he was not particularly interested.

His job was to work with the subversive elements in the capitals of the world and light fires. After Paris, London, or Cairo, Tokyo was a piece of cake, but he took no chances.

He walked silently over to the bed and looked down at the woman who lay there. She still looked young to him, but he did not care. He held his hand in front of her face and felt her breath. She was fast asleep.

He walked over to the window; it would be light in about thirty minutes. He then picked up a large crystal ball she had on her desk. Of course he was wearing gloves, so he did not leave any fingerprints, but even if he did, the house would be on fire soon and all the evidence would be destroyed. He walked over to her wardrobe and selected a black woolen coat. He recognized it as being tweed from his native Scotland, and he knew that it would burn well. If he left the crystal ball on top of it, he knew that it would take less than an hour for the sun's rays to set it on fire.

He went back to the desk, and it was then that he realized something was wrong. He had been told that the crystal ball would be on a late-nineteenth-century art nouveau stand, fashioned to look like three frogs, but that was not where he had found it. He took out a miniature flashlight and looked around. The ball had been removed from the stand and had been left on a sheet of black paper from which he had just lifted it. Someone else had been there before him to make the same preparations, and he considered it a personal blow to his pride.

When the sun came up, its rays would be focused through the crystal ball onto the black paper, and soon a curl of white smoke would appear, which would grow until flames started to lick the furniture. A number of perfume bottles had been knocked over next to the paper, and he realized now that it had been the alcohol in the perfume that he had smelled when he entered the room.

He took out the sheet of solid fuel he had brought with him and slipped it under the black paper. Then he checked the position of the crystal ball again to make sure it would catch the first rays of sunlight as they crept into the room. He read the label on the ball, which was written in English, warning that if it was removed from its stand, it may pose a fire risk. What he could not decipher was the writing on the sheet of paper under a paperweight on the desk.

If he was to leave it where it was, it would be burned in the fire, so he picked it up and slipped it into his pocket. It was taboo to take anything from the scene of a job, but he felt that he needed something to show to his client to explain what had happened here, so he did not have any choice.

As he left the room, he again looked over at the woman sleeping in the bed. She had left a night light on by her bed, and he could see her face quite clearly. He had been told that she took sleeping pills regularly and that at this time of night she would be fast asleep, so there would be no need to inject her with a drug.

It occurred to him suddenly that the letter on the desk might be a suicide note, but if that was so, why would she leave it there where no one would ever see it? He guessed that she had taken a large dose of sleeping pills and would never know when the fire started, but he could not understand why she should want to commit suicide in so complicated a manner. He supposed that she wanted the fire to destroy her body after she died so nobody else would be able to see it, but he could never understand the way Orientals thought. He would never choose to die in a fire. When he was still a child, he had seen the body of someone who had died in a napalm attack, and the sight had made him quite sick. Ever since, he had always tried to avoid looking at the bodies of fire victims.

He changed his mind again and put the letter back on top of the desk. He could not understand these people's customs, but it had nothing to do with him, and it was taboo to take anything away from a job.

He closed the door behind him and concentrated on making a clean getaway without anyone seeing him. He did not give another thought to the strange fire rituals of these Orientals.

2   *The Murderer*

The widow removed the needle from the record, and having stopped listening to the aria, she went back to her own practice. Since her husband and son had died, it had been her love of opera that had kept her so fit, both physically and mentally, to the ripe age of eighty-one.

If she had not been able to join the various characters and sing of love and hatred, she never would have been able to wait twenty-six years for her revenge without doing something that she would regret later. She could not count the number of times that she had thought of going to kill that woman with her own hands. She still had the pistol she had been given fifty years ago when she went to Italy to study, and there was also the poison that her father, who had been a war criminal, had received from the Nazis when he visited Germany before the war.

Her schoolfriends had all envied her for having married such a successful businessman, but she had never thought of herself as lucky. As a child she had dreamed of becoming a world-famous opera singer, but when she married she had been forced to abandon her dream. She had devoted herself to raising their only child, but when he grew up, he had inherited her artistic side and had refused to join his father's company, preferring instead to go to Paris and try to become a painter. When he was there, he learned how limited his talent was, and he ended up marrying some cheap little Japanese girl. She would have been happier if he had just had a child by a French prostitute, as the child would have grown up by now and might have become a famous tenor like Yoshie Fujiwara, who had foreign blood. There was nothing like foreign blood, especially for an opera singer.

She paused and dreamed of having a blond-haired grandson playing Pinkerton on the stage in Paris while she played Madame Butterfly awaiting his return. These pleasant thoughts continued for a minute, and then they disappeared to be replaced by her hatred for that woman.

When she stole my son's love, she took away my only happiness, the old woman thought bitterly. *She said she had gone to Paris to study child care, so why did she marry a second-rate artist like my son? She could only have been after his money. I married the man that my parents arranged for me, and I wanted to have as many children as possible, but after my first son, I had to have my womb removed, and so he was all the more precious to us. She tricked him. When he realized that he was not cut out to become a painter, he would have come home, taken over his father's company, and married a suitable girl from a good home. He was only having a brief fling before he settled down, but that woman . . . she stole his whole future. That would have been forgivable, but why did she have to kill him?*

I did my best to break up their marriage. That is why I arranged for the nurse to sleep with him. She had refused to let him into her bed. He told me that himself, so I know it was true. The doctor told me that his disease sometimes made patients more sexually active than normal, and I only did what I thought was best for him. Of course, I did hope I would be able to drive her crazy with jealousy. I had hoped she would become so incensed that she would kill the nurse. I would not have put something like that past her. I had imagined that it would be something like an opera wherein the heroine, driven to a fury by jealousy, kills her rival, but no, that damn woman had to kill my son instead.

I had hoped she would kill the nurse, and then, while she was in prison, I would take my son and grandson into my care and treat them to the love they deserved.

When I heard that my son had died, I knew straightaway that it was that woman's work, but no matter how often I told the police, they said they could not do anything without proof. I thought I would punish her then and there, but then I realized that would be too easy for her. I wanted her to taste the same pain and despair that I had.

When I learned that her son was another man's and not my son's, I was delighted and waited for him to grow. I knew that God was helping me make my revenge.

I decided to sit back and wait for her son to grow before I would take my revenge, and in the meantime I made all my plans and preparations. After that, my life really seemed worth living. I sat and watched the strife that grew between them with pleasure, and every now and then I would let the son know that his mother had killed her husband, just to keep things on the boil until I was ready to open the curtain on my little plot.

That woman, her son, and his friends probably all thought it was just coincidence, but in reality, it was all a web of fate that I had woven over the years with patience and money. Everybody acted according to my plan, just like good characters in an opera. Even the bit-part actors did what they were supposed to do, and, although they had me worried sometimes, it was worth all the money and risk.

Of course, I could never have managed it without the woman with the lion, the fire eater, or the foreign consultant. My father's friend had connections with the underworld, and the men that his consultant introduced were one hundred percent reliable. They did everything they were paid for. Most of all, however, I have to thank the nurse who made the fireman do everything that I planned for him. I discovered her myself, and I was not wrong in my choice. She may come from a poor family, but she is a born actress, and when she told the fireman that she was the daughter of my son, she really seemed to be living the part. I knew that he would not be able to refuse her if he thought he had seen the moment of his lover's creation, but what a part. . . . I had not really wanted to kill him, but the consultant said he was asking too many questions and that it would be dangerous to let him live.

He may have been branded an arsonist, but surely he could not complain. He had plunged into the burning building after his love like a hero on the stage, and he had died believing that his love was true.

But now my revenge is complete. The day when I make that

woman pay is here. My consultant sent me his best man to break into her room, inject her with a sedative, and place the crystal ball so it would set the house on fire. My son sent it to me when he first went abroad, before he got mixed up with that woman, and after he died, I sent it to her saying that next time she was going to kill someone, she should use that and not torment some poor dog by setting its tail on fire. She did not say a word, but I am sure she must have been shocked to realize that I knew everything.

When I heard she had had the nerve to keep it on her desk, I made up my mind that I would use it when I had her killed, and I had a call from the consultant just now to tell me that everything has gone according to plan. That woman is finally dead, killed by fire just as my son was. I feel so happy that I could sing this aria like I have never sung it before, but I am told there is a policeman here to see me. I wonder what he wants.

3   The Murderer

Michitaro's grandmother had the Chief Inspector shown into the reception room with the grand piano in it. Although he had aged quite considerably in the last twenty-six years, she could still see in him the young station chief who had investigated her son's death. Compared to him, she thought she had aged very little. She had grown a little hard of hearing, but she was much more vivacious than she had been when her husband was still alive. She had spent the intervening years thinking about her daughter-in-law, that woman who had stolen her son, thinking how she would be punished. It had given meaning to her life, and that was why her skin was still so fresh looking.

More than anything, it was the fact that this policeman had chosen to help that woman that she had felt the need to teach her a lesson. She realized now, for the first time, that she had felt attracted to this young policeman, but that woman, not content with taking her son, had also stolen this man's affections.

But that was all finished now. God had finally punished her and had brought this policeman back to her. She had made various plans for him over the years, and she had arranged it so that when he left the police force, he would get a job as the chief investigator at the insurance company.

"Thank you for all the trouble you went to on my grandson's behalf."

"Not at all. I am only sorry that we have not been able to catch his murderer yet."

"I hardly think there is much chance of that," she said, and putting her hand over her mouth, she laughed throatily.

She had already heard from her consultant that the people who had dealt with that side of the job had left the country, and she had seen to it that they were well paid for their work. She wanted to tell him the whole story, and it was all she could do to hold the words back.

"No, I am sure we will catch them sooner or later. We have found the car and discovered that it was rented by a foreigner. He has already left the country, but we have asked Interpol to get him for us."

He explained everything in a quiet voice, and she realized that he had not changed at all in the last twenty-six years after all. He still did not show any emotion.

"The reason I am here today has to do with Michitaro's mother. May I offer my condolences."

"No. Don't talk to me of that woman. I don't want to hear anything about the woman who killed my son. She got what was due to her, that's all. When I heard that she, too, had died in a fire, I wanted to pray and thank God for giving her what she deserved."

Her face became twisted with rage, and she had to force herself to hide it and assume her usual prima donna demeanor.

"Actually, just before Michitaro's mother died, in fact I think it was the morning of the same day, I received a personal letter from her saying that the people who had kidnapped Michitaro had also threatened to kill her. She said that she thought they intended to do it that night, and while she wanted the police to protect her, the person who had hired the killers was a very close relative and she did not know what she should do."

"That is a very roundabout way of saying that it was me, but she only did it to malign me. It is quite unforgivable!"

She was so angry that she spoke with the full power that years of training as an opera singer had given her.

"Of course I did not believe it either," the Inspector said coolly, clasping his hands behind his back. "Nevertheless, we arrested a man a few hours ago, a foreigner, whom we followed after he left her house a short while before it burned down. He chose to use his right of silence and has not spoken a word, but wouldn't you know, he was carrying a sheet of writing paper, and he says that he found it on a desk in the house."

As soon as she heard this, her pulse quickened. Something had obviously gone wrong, but the consultant had told her that even if one of the men was caught, it would never be traced back to her.

"We checked the handwriting. It definitely belongs to Yoriko, and it would appear to be a suicide note. I have a copy of it here. Would you like to see it?"

He held out the copy for her, but when she showed no inclination to take it, he started to read it to her.

" 'Now that I have had my beloved son taken from me, I have decided to take my own life. I have just taken a large dose of sleeping pills, but before I die I would like to admit to my crime twenty-six years ago. I killed my husband and then set fire to the house. I know that in a few hours this note will be burned together with this house and that nobody will ever see it, but I feel I have to put this in writing once before I die. I have put the crystal ball my mother-in-law gave me on a piece of black velvet and connected a piece of black cotton from there to a bottle of benzene, so when the sun comes up in the morning, this house, my body, my crime, and my memories will all be burned away.'

"After that, she has written the date and signed her name."

"It's a lie! It's impossible! That woman would never take her own life. It is quite out of the question."

She started to shake with rage, but the Inspector just stood quietly and watched her.

It couldn't happen. Nothing so stupid could happen. I have spent the last twenty-six years writing the script for a great opera, and I can't let the last scene be wrecked like this, she thought.

"You're wrong, there is no way that woman would choose to kill herself. I hired someone to do it. I punished her.

233

She killed my beloved son, and so I had her suffer the same fate and had her burned. I did it. . . . I planned it all. I told her son that she was a murderer and an arsonist. When he was still in junior high school, I telephoned him and sent him letters to let him know, and look what happened. No sooner did he find out than he started doing it, too. He was not my son's child. He was the son of some man she met somewhere.

"I arranged for that lion and its owner to be brought to Japan, too. Her husband, the Frenchman, was my son's real child, but before I could arrange for him to come to Japan, he died in an accident. I made sure that his wife was given plenty of money, but she tried to extort some more out of me, so I had her killed. I had her killed and then had them make the lion eat that fireman's I.D. I had to make people remember the fire that killed my son."

She wanted to say more, but suddenly she felt faint. Was she doing the right thing to tell him all this?

"Was it you who ordered all those fires, too? So it wasn't the work of Michitaro, was it?"

"I wouldn't know about that, but I heard a story from a friend of mine who is in the real estate business, about an area that was up for redevelopment, but the old people who lived there refused to move. They lived in some dirty old city-owned apartments, but they said they didn't want to move because the area had too many memories for them. They organized a protest movement to get the plan dropped.

"Old people are really pitiful, aren't they? If you want to get on, you must be like me and stay one step ahead of the young, not worry about the past. I went and talked to them, but they wouldn't listen to me either, and so, the story has it, an expert on arson was brought in from abroad to burn the buildings down. Of course, some of the old people died in the fires, but the more who died the more people there would be who would see the need for a high-rise development."

She knew she had said more than she should and that she must pull herself together, but she felt very weak and her legs were unsteady. She could not believe that the woman would actually kill herself. She should never have waited all these years. She should have killed her right away, killed her with her own hand. How ironic it was. There she was thinking that she had finally managed to punish her, but that woman had beaten her to it and made her victory hollow.

All of a sudden she felt that she wanted to sing an aria, to put all her hatred and her desire for revenge into words, but what was the name of that song? What were the Italian lyrics? She was always singing it, but for some reason she could not remember it. What was the first note? The first word? She just could not remember. Oh yes, "Black angel of revenge, fly to me." That was it, the finale of the third act of *Medea*.

She took a step forward, and her whole body swayed. Suddenly there was a piercing pain in her heart.

She thought she had forgotten something important . . . the payment for the foreign specialist? No, that was not it. The bouquet for the Italian tenor who would be performing that night? No, it was nothing like that. Oh yes, the nurse . . . that clever little nurse. She had forgotten to put her into her will. She had had all the papers drawn up, but she had forgotten to sign them. It was a shame. She had been a complete stranger, but she had done everything that she was asked without comment. She had even played the part of her granddaughter beautifully. But it was too late now, she could not do any more. Darkness was waiting for her, and there was nothing she could do to keep it away.

3   *The Detective*

The Chief Inspector crumpled the copy of the suicide note in his pocket as he left the old woman's room. There was no doubt that the copy had been directly responsible for the old woman's heart attack. It had been vastly more effective than he had ever hoped it would be. In fact it could almost be called a murder weapon, because there was no doubt that it had killed just as effectively as a gun.

He wondered if she would have realized that it was a fake if she had looked at it. He had written it himself, and it had been very difficult for him to sound convincing when he read it. After all he was a policeman, not an actor. Judging by the effect, however, he had not done a bad job. She just could not bear the thought that her victim had managed to escape her revenge by killing herself.

When they had arrested the foreigner after the fire, he knew straightaway that it was the work of the old woman. Not only was it typical of the kind of thing he could expect from her, there was also that note he had received from Michitaro's mother in which she stated quite clearly that she thought her mother-in-law was going to kill her. The only problem was that he did not have any way of proving any of it, and it was then that he had a brainstorm.

He knew it was her pride and her desire for revenge that had kept her alive all these years, and if he were to tell her that all her plans had failed and that her victim had taken her own life, the old woman would lose her reason for living.

That was when he had faked the suicide note, and as a result the old woman had told him more than even he had ever hoped for, bringing him that much closer to the truth. More than that, however, he was pleased to be able to help his love. He realized that, with all her wealth, the old woman had been too powerful for Yoriko alone, but with his help they had been able to topple her. He knew that it was basically a family problem between Yoriko and her mother-in-law, and he had no right involving himself in it, but it was also his job to know the truth.

Anyway, he had finally managed to do something very unpolicemanlike before he retired. As he crumpled the copy of the note into a ball, he wondered if it could be called murder.

It had all begun twenty-six years ago, when she had found out that he was not going to arrest her daughter-in-law. She had summoned him to Kaenji Temple.

"If you do not arrest that murderess, I will punish her myself. I will make her burn, too, and avenge my son. And let me warn you, if you take her side in all this, you cannot expect to do very well in your chosen career. I have a lot of friends, you know, both in politics and in the police force. Close friends who would be very willing to do me a favor."

Her threatening him like this only made him feel more sympathetic toward the artist's young widow.

"You say you have no proof and there are no witnesses,

but God knows what she has done and so does this dog. He cannot speak, but he saw everything."

She showed him a small statue of the terrier that had died in the fire and hugged it as if it were alive.

"This dog will punish her for what she has done one day. The name of the murderer is engraved on its stomach."

She then showed him the sutra she had copied and made him read what she had written in the request part. He could no longer quite recall what it had been, but he remembered thinking that what she was doing was no different than sticking pins in a wax effigy, typical of losers throughout history. As time passed, however, he learned that her threats had not been entirely empty, as he started to drop behind the other elite officers who had joined the force with him.

When he learned that Ikuo Onda's I.D. had been found in the stomach of the lion, his thoughts went back to the meeting in the temple, and he guessed straightaway that it was the work of the old woman. Ikuo's name had been engraved on his mind all these years, and he had never forgotten it.

Those children had given him a hard time. They had all looked him straight in the eye and said they had seen a batlike man breathing fire. He had not believed them, though, and even now he believed they had been responsible for the fire. He did not know which of them was directly responsible, but he was convinced that the cause had been the children playing with fire. He didn't think the painter had been murdered at all. He had just been late in making his escape. These artistic types were all the same. No doubt he had been sitting around drinking wine all afternoon and had been drunk when the fire broke out.

He remembered how Michitaro's mother had lain in his embrace, her face streaked with tears, and said, "You believe me, don't you? I did not kill my husband or set the house on fire, but his mother seems to be convinced that I did, and she goes down to the police station every day to try to make them arrest me."

They had been lying in a hotel bed and the radio had been playing "The Kiss of Fire," a tango that was very popular at the time. If she had really taken her own life, instead of being killed, it would make the whole episode much more romantic. He had given up his career in order to protect his lover who was guilty of murder, but as it was, it had been a waste. He had not been able to do anything for her.

He had a pang of guilty conscience and wondered if he had really fabricated the suicide note for her. Hadn't he done it to get back at the old woman for standing in the way of his promotion? Hadn't this just been a way of making her pay before he retired?

He knew that he should not have intervened in what was really only a squabble between in-laws. His own wife and mother did not get on very well, and his mother refused to live with them, preferring to live in one of the dirty old city-owned apartments that the old woman had complained about. That was why he had been very interested when she had talked of a foreign gang being brought in to torch the old buildings. He guessed that she had got the story wrong somehow. He did not believe that anyone would actually go to such lengths to make people move, but the insurance company had been investing heavily in real estate recently, and she might have heard something from one of her colleagues.

It would be worth his getting the whole story from the foreign arsonist, if only for his mother's sake. But he did not want anything more to do with arson and murder in that family. He would leave it all to Ryosaku. He was sure the younger man would find out the truth in the end. Who had lit the fires? Why had Ikuo died? Who had kidnapped Michitaro and then killed him? Who had killed his mother? He knew that it would take a long time to find out, but he was prepared to wait.

He thought about the job he had been offered with the insurance company. He knew he would never get another offer like it, but he was not sure if he wanted to work for a company after he left the force. He had always had a secret desire to write a book based on his experience in the force, and judging by the way the suicide note he had written had been received, he felt that he might have a talent for writing.

5   The Murderer

The nurse went up onto the deserted roof of the hospital, and sitting down on a bench there, lit a cigarette.

She had started to smoke originally in order to annoy Ikuo, but now, a year later, she had become a heavy smoker. She blew a smoke ring, and as she watched it rise up into the blue sky, she realized that she had really done it. She was rich.

I did everything the old woman asked. I don't know how she could be so accurate in predicting Ikuo's reactions, but I only had to do what she said, so it was easy. The only thing that had not been in any of her plans was the appearance of that detective.

He really loved me. Ikuo felt the same way, but he always seemed to suspect me of something. That detective is a bit simple. He lost his wife and the child she was carrying, but he still believes in the simple things in life. He told me he wanted to marry me and to have children, but I wonder what he would say if he knew that I had been on the pill all this time.

I don't want to marry a poor detective and have his children, anyway, and now I won't have to. I am rich. There cannot be many people in Japan of my age who are as rich as I am. The accountant told me that if I was to sell all the stock in the insurance company, it would be worth several billion yen. I will keep it all in a Swiss bank, and then travel the world playing the part of her granddaughter, which she gave me.

I should raise my glass to the man who had promised to marry me but then left me for another girl. He taught me that there was no such thing as eternal love. It only lasts as long as you lie to each other, but nobody believes that, which is why they are always disappointed. I don't believe in eternal love, though. That is why I am free. I can have blond lovers, black lovers, lovers of all kinds, and when I have finished with one, I can just move on to the next.

With my looks and that old woman's money, they will flock to me, and I will be able to have any man that I want. They will always be the ones who are fooled, and I will be the one who is fooling them. I don't want to spend my whole life with just one man and devote myself to raising his children. I want to enjoy myself and live life to the fullest.

I never knew my father. My mother had a different man every week, but she still was not happy. I don't want to be like her, and I don't want to spend the rest of my life pretending to be a little angel and looking after invalids. But the doctor says there is a chance the old woman might live. She really clings to life, and thanks to all her opera singing she is in quite good shape. She could live for another ten years, and then my youth would be gone. My youth is all I have, and I could not bear the thought of flirting with men at fifty like my mother did.

She cannot really expect to go on singing these stupid operas for another ten years after having a heart attack. I won't let her. I never did like opera. All that talk of love, hate, and revenge. It is stupid to go on loving or hating someone for years. There is no point in it.

You should live for today. There may never be a tomorrow. If anyone knows that, I do. I have seen all those people in their death beds every day, clutching their bank books and regretting that they did not use their money while they could.

The old woman showed me the documents, which made me her heir, and the lawyer and accountant witnessed them. If she was to live for another ten years, she might change her mind. It will be easy for me to do it. I did it to her grandson, and this time it will be even easier. I am her private nurse. No one need ever know. All I have to do is put a bubble of air in her drip feed, and it will be all over. It will be for her own good. Even if she were to live for another ten years, she would forget the words of her operas and would not be able to hear her own voice.

The cigarette had burned down to her fingers, so she dropped it on the ground and stamped it out. She looked down and counted the cigarette ends. It had taken her five cigarettes to make up her mind to turn off Michitaro's life-support apparatus, but this time it had taken only two.

EPILOGUE

A selection of articles from recent newspapers, which tell the rest of the story:

OBITUARY

Michitaro Matsubara (Executive of C.D. Insurance Company. Aged 31.)

Of heart failure at 2:15 P.M. on the twenty-second. The grandson of the founder of the C.D. Insurance Company, he was involved in a hit-and-run accident at approximately 2 A.M. on the morning of the twentieth. He was rushed to the Junshindo University Hospital but died without regaining consciousness. A memorial service was held at his home in the Seijo District and his mother was the chief mourner.

Maiyu Newspaper

Ikuo Onda (Fireman of the Seijo fire station. Aged 31.)

A funeral was held for Mr. Onda at the Onjiin Temple on the twenty-first. The union claims that he died in performance of his duty and says that his family should receive compensation. They will continue to protest until they get satisfaction.

Provincial Union News

Yoriko Matsubara. (Professor at Oyunohara Women's College. Aged 56.)

Mrs. Matsubara died recently at a fire in her home and a memorial service was held for her at the university, which was attended by many of her students and friends. Mrs. Matsubara is best known for the methods of psychological testing that she developed.

Oyunohara University Hospital

Toyo Matsubara (President of C.D. Insurance Company.)

Mrs. Matsubara died of respiratory problems at 4:30 P.M. on the fifth at the St. Magdalene Hospital, aged 81.

Her estate was valued at several billion yen, but as she did not leave any heirs, the money will be used to construct the Matsubara Memorial Opera Hall as she requested while she was still alive.

Asayomi Newspaper

Her husband is a detective in the homicide division!

Chieko Minamibara, who retired recently from the surgical ward, married her fiancé, Ryosaku Uno, aged 31. He says that while he has no money, he wants to have as many children as possible. His bride seemed to be very embarrassed and did not make any comment.

Nurse's Monthly

Chief Inspector Edogawa, who retired from the force recently, refused several offers of employment, saying,

"I have had enough of desk work. I want to get a place in the country and work as a farmer while I write a detective novel. Of course, it will be concerned with arson, and I intend to call it *The Kiss of Fire*. I hope nobody thinks it is a pornographic book!" he added with a laugh.

Police Gazette